The White Mountain Murders

Also by Steve Sherman

The Maple Sugar Murders

The White Mountain Murders

Steve Sherman

Walker and Company
New York

First published in the United States of America in 1989 by Walker Publishing Company, Inc.

Published simultaneously in Canada by Thomas Allen & Son Canada, Limited, Markham, Ontario.

Library of Congress Cataloging-in-Publication Data
Sherman, Steve, 1938–
The White Mountain murders.

I. Title.
PS3569.H4337W47   1989   813'.54   88-27757
ISBN 0-8027-5735-9

Printed in the United States of America.

10 9 8 7 6 5 4 3 2 1

1

FIRST WE KILL THE LAWYERS.
—WILLIAM SHAKESPEARE

HUGH QUINT DROVE north from Arcadia because Miles Cooper phoned and said, "I got something this time that'll triple your money. Triple it! So what do you think?"

"Well, I don't know," Hugh said. "What're you talking about?"

"I'm talking about tripling your money, that's what I'm talking about."

"No, I mean *what's* going to triple my money?"

"Come on up and I'll show you. It's fantastic. This is the greatest one ever, I'm telling you. This one is IT!"

"Miles, just tell me. It's a long way up there."

"An hour."

"Three hours."

"See? Triple!"

Hugh shook his head and smiled, knowing that Miles Cooper was cocking his ear to every telephonic nuance he could catch. "You're telling me to empty my wallet on something you won't tell me about. Come on."

"I need more than five bucks, Hugh. We're talking big bucks here once I get the prototype finished and over to G.E. How does G.E. Sound to you?"

"Great, but G.E. makes its own stuff."

"Whatever. The thing is, you got to see it."

"Bring it down here."

"Can't. Bad tires, *flat* tires. Flatter than a witch's lip."

1

"Fix them."

"I can't drive all the way down there on a bad clutch."

"Right, Miles."

"Just come on up. That's all I'm asking."

"Tell me what it is, will you?"

He whispered his reply with his mouth obviously pressed close to the phone. "You know I can't do that."

"Paranoia," Hugh sang.

Back to full voice: "Yeah, well, *you* lost any ideas lately?"

"Nobody is tapping the lines. Nobody is going to steal your ideas."

"This one they'll steal. This is *it*. Come on up. You can be a leaf peeper. It's the good season. Have a nice day and all that. Plus you get to see something amazing. What's an hour?"

Hugh sighed.

"Aristotle would come up."

"All right, Miles, but I'm not bringing money."

"Never make promises you'll regret breaking when you see this one."

So Hugh drove north.

By the time he reached Longfield, the sun was high and Hugh was feeling the draw of the mighty White Mountains up ahead. Sleek Interstate 93 wound alongside the glacier-cut valleys and deep into the tightening notches that sliced the range. Late September was changing the steep forests to reds and oranges, yellows and browns, igniting the hillsides in benign flames—another annual autumn miracle. This was the time of year when three million gawkers came to northern New England to parade by confetti hills and valleys that existed nowhere else on earth in such profusion and variety.

Longfield lay in the shallows of a vast wind-bent meadow, funneling to an Ice Age crevice in the Whites—a

2

monumental sight, packed with greed-inspiring tourism potential for the trinket-and-trash trade. Luckily, the residing locals had long ago outlawed such outsiders with ornery town ordinances, allowing tourist towns like Lincoln and Conway down the road to reap the rewards of noisy plastic come-ons and fast-food eat stations. Longfield kept its long fields intact and uncluttered, its peaks soaring at the tail end of a billboardless, roadless vista. Longfield was content to make its fortune on postcards.

Longfield itself was more a village than a full-fledged town—white steeple church with abandoned carriage stalls in the rear, granite slab steps for the white houses with black shutters, maple-lined Main Street with no parking meters, red brick schoolhouse, baseball diamond, diner with backless stools. Yield signs outnumbered Stop signs. Hugh liked it.

He liked Miles Cooper too, but a few hours of liking Miles Cooper lasted weeks; or, if Hugh was lucky, months. The last time he'd seen Miles, Hugh had ended up investing a thousand dollars in a process for manufacturing waterproof books for people who liked to read in bathtubs. In the end, he'd written it off as mental health maintenance for both of them.

He remembered the time Miles had worked up a scheme for imprinting snapshots on bay windows. The idea was to update medieval stained-glass windows to modern-day photography. First, you picked a window in your house. Then you covered the window with his special translucent laminate. Then you projected a color slide onto the laminate and his special secret chemical reactions transferred the slide projection to the laminate, thereby creating a personalized stained-glass window in your own home. Think of the number of families with windows in the country, he told Hugh, think how many pictures the old man was always taking of the kids and the dog and mountaintops. This way they didn't have to send off to some laboratory for those giant poster enlargements, then frame them and take up wall space—all that stuff. They could install Miles's WindoPhoto instead. He hadn't yet come up with the exact chemical combination, but he was working on it.

Hugh turned into the sand-dirt driveway of the Cooper homestead—a late-eighteenth-century masterpiece with four brick chimneys, fieldstone foundation, and narrow clapboards thickened by one generation of white paint after another. An unmowed hay field spread around the house, and the ever-present White Mountains loomed into the crisp, blue sky. Deer country. Hugh steered toward the driveway extension that led to the edge of the woods and the site of Miles's reconverted barn and brain center.

Miles burst through the screen door in the main house to stop Hugh from going to the barn. He skipped down the wooden steps of the wraparound porch with his characteristic rush of greeting. Big wave, big smile. They shook hands, Miles on the pumping end. Then he pulled Hugh closer.

"I got to tell you," he said, glancing at the house, conspiring, "Mother thinks you're here because of Amy, so don't be surprised. I'll explain later."

"What about Amy?"

"I'll explain later."

Sarah Cooper stepped to the edge of the porch. The screen door slammed behind her. She was smiling and wringing her hands in her blue-striped apron, waiting for them to hurry up and come in.

Hugh waved to her and she returned the gesture, happy to see him, her upright rounded figure topped with grandmotherly gray.

"Hi, Sarah!" he called.

"She thinks I talked to you about something else, something about Amy," Miles said under his breath, camouflag-

4

ing the message with smiles and operatic extravagance. "So don't blame me for anything, okay?"

Sarah led them into the front room and toward the shiny maple dining table with its long, narrow white runner hanging over both ends. The prized Dunlap high chest stood against a showcase wall, in center command of the other charming but decidedly less high-quality furniture.

Sarah had passed on her moony cheeks to Miles, along with her effusive energy, and her tendency to keep everybody else's keel angled in her direction. What she kept for herself were two petite dimples that showed when she smiled, deep blue eyes, a pug nose that could surprise an Eskimo, and a bent for wearing some shade or other of efficient household blue at all times and occasions.

She also wouldn't take no for an answer in the queendom of her kitchen.

"Now, Hugh," she said, before sitting, "you didn't eat any lunch, did you?"

"As a matter of fact . . ."

"I thought so," she said, moving to the kitchen, "so I'm going to fix you up a little something right now."

"Sarah, I was going to say that I did stop for something."

"Oh, road food," she called over her shoulder in a civil tone. But, by the way she clicked her tongue, she apparently considered it totally contemptible. "That's no food at all. You stay right there."

"Really, Sarah, I don't need anything."

"Yes, you do. You look too thin. Women don't like men too skinny."

"Mother," Miles called after her, "he doesn't want anything."

"I know what he wants. Now you two talk. I can hear you."

"I wish you wouldn't, Sarah."

"Yes, you do," she called, putting a pan on a stove burner.

"Well, not too much then."

5

"I know how much you want, Hugh dear. You just go right on and talk with Miles while I fix something up."

"Don't go to any trouble."

"I'm only going to heat up a little noon soup and a piece of apple pie. I'm really glad you came up, Hugh. I've been so worried."

Hugh looked to Miles for translation, but he only fluttered his fingers in mock concern.

"Miles told you about Amy," she called through the doorway.

Hugh looked at Miles again and spread his hands in question. Miles shrugged and turned to the kitchen.

"I'll have some pie too, Mother," he announced.

"I know you will," she said to her little boy who had voted in the last four presidential elections. "And you'll have some soup too. You can't let Hugh sit there and eat alone. Miles, you set the table. And don't think I don't know that you rushed back from town to eat with Hugh."

He set the table, and Sarah Cooper the cook brought in two gigantic bowls of steaming vegetable soup, then returned with a platter of thick crusty homemade bread and two glasses of milk, and returned yet again with two huge wedges of warm apple pie topped with slices of Vermont cheddar.

"You did it again, Sarah," Hugh said, because he'd had Sarah Cooper's apple pies before. Sarah Cooper never served an apple pie old, which meant four hours from the oven. Tarts were served old, pies by definition were *fresh*, still oven-warm, never reheated. Their crusts had to be half sweet butter for flavor, half shortening for flakiness, and all bumpy with heaps of thick slices inside that held their shape, like first-class Northern Spy sweet and tart apples—no mushy MacIntoshes. Add some allspice, a touch of mace, and Sarah's secret balance of sugar and sweet butter chunks, and the outcome was inevitably and aromatically supreme.

6

"You drink that milk, Hugh dear," she said, sitting down, businesslike. "It's good for you. You can't drink whiskey all the time."

"Mother, Hugh doesn't drink *whiskey*."

"I know what he drinks. It's all the same to me anyway."

They ate while Sarah watched. Hugh looked up and smiled, but Miles ate nonstop, eyes avoiding his mother and Hugh.

"Now," Sarah said after proper delay, "do you think Amy's all right?"

Hugh glanced at Miles, who kept his spoon revolving from bowl to mouth, eyes down, shoulders hunched. "Well, yes, I think so. She should be. Actually, Sarah, to tell you the truth, I'm not sure what you mean."

"But Miles told you. You came up here." Then she turned to the revolving-spoon man next to her and stared, first with unbelieving eyes and then with hot ones. "Miles!" she snapped, clipping the name like a carrot chopper.

He kept the spoon going.

"Didn't you tell him about Amy?"

"I told him," he said, looking up finally. "I told him I'd explain it. I'm doing it right now. He's here, isn't he?"

"She's your sister and you didn't tell him?"

"I'm going to tell him right now. I wanted to tell him in person, so here he is, Mother. There, right there, he's eating your soup."

Sarah stared at him as he flattened his palm across the table again and again toward Hugh. "She's your sister, Miles," she said. "What did you tell him?"

"He's up here, Mother, see, right there, right there in front of us. She's my half-sister."

Sarah turned to Hugh. "What did he tell you? I know what he told you."

What did one do amid such an exchange? One demurred. Hugh demurred, surrendering his hands in

7

neutrality, keeping silent, keeping out of it.

She turned back to Miles. "You told him about that scheme of yours, didn't you?"

"Mother!"

"Your sister's in trouble and all you can think of is yourself!" She turned to Hugh. "I don't know what kind of son I have. I just don't know."

"What about Amy?" Hugh asked.

She turned back to Miles but spoke to Hugh. "All he does is think about *his* life, about his crazy schemes."

"They're not crazy," Miles said.

"If he'd do things the way they're supposed to be done," she said, still facing Miles and talking to Hugh, "he'd accomplish something maybe. But, oh no, he has to think up new ways to do everything. It's just an excuse not to work. Look at that field out there. It needs mowing!"

Hugh reached for Sarah's hand. "What about Amy?"

She took a deep breath and sniffed out the pollen of anger. "She's been missing for three days, and I'm just worried to death about her."

"She's been gone before," Miles said. "Nothing's wrong. She goes off, that's all. That's what I was going to tell you."

Sarah's gaze simmered hot at Miles.

"I was going to tell him. You didn't give me a chance. He wouldn't have come up if I'd told him that. He'd have said give her a couple more days and then call back. Wouldn't you, Hugh?"

Better to shrug, which Hugh did. "You haven't heard from her at all?"

"No," she said, wringing her fingers together. "It's not like her."

"Yes, it is," Miles said, sliding his hand across the table to wipe the slate clean. "Listen, if Amy was really *missing*, I'd be worried, but she's not really missing. We just haven't heard from her."

"That new chief won't do anything," Sarah said. "He's

8

too young, he doesn't have a family of his own, so he doesn't understand. I told him about Amy, and he said he couldn't do anything. He wouldn't, that's all. Just wouldn't."

When Sarah sighed and looked away, Hugh and Miles glanced at each other in search of what to say next.

"But you'll help, won't you, Hugh dear?" she said, looking back and smiling.

"Sure, I will. She's probably someplace where . . ."

"Oh," Sarah said and got up to answer the phone. "Now *eat*, Hugh, you finish that pie."

Miles stretched his hand toward the other room. "See!" he called after her. "Two to one that's her right now. We're sitting here talking about her and she calls. It happens all the time. That's her, Mother. That's Amy!"

They watched her go into her bedroom for the phone. Then Hugh leaned across the table and said, "Miles, why the hell didn't you tell me?"

"How can I tell you something like that on the phone?"

"Words. They work every time."

"Listen, a pine needle drops on Amy and Mother has her in the Mayo Clinic for three months. Don't worry about it."

"*She's* worrying about it."

"Eat, eat," said Miles, grinning, boy truant, diversionary tactician.

"You're the one who better clean up the crumbs or you're in the pot out there."

Sarah appeared at the doorway and leaned against the wall. She slid an apprehensive hand to her throat. The hollow look on her face silenced the two men staring toward her. "That was . . ."

When she didn't finish, Hugh said, "What is it?"

"I knew something like this would happen."

"What?"

"Bryan's dead."

9

2

HE THAT LIES WITH DOGS RISETH WITH FLEAS.

—GEORGE HERBERT

THEY WAITED FOR her to continue. When she didn't, Hugh asked, "What happened?"

Sarah blinked back to where she was and said, "I don't know."

"It was a heart attack," Miles said. "The old guy got a heart attack."

"Oh, you never liked him, ever since he drew up that will," she said, her head shaking no.

"That's not true at all, and you know it."

"I know no such thing."

Miles looked to Hugh for relief, but what could you say when heat was piled on anguish? The three of them gazed everywhere but at each other until finally Hugh asked, "Was it a heart attack, Sarah?"

She shook her head. "I don't know who could do such a thing."

Miles couldn't keep his mouth shut. "He was a lawyer," he told Hugh, with heavy emphasis on "lawyer," the word gilded with scorn.

"He was *our* lawyer, and don't you forget it. He was an attorney."

Miles spread his hands and supplicated heaven.

"You and your schemes."

"Mother, all I said was . . ."

"I know what you said and I know what you meant,

10

Miles Cooper. I know you. Ever since that will."

"He made you do it."

"He made me do no such thing."

"He put it into your head."

"He did not."

"I saw him put it into your head, I saw him."

"You saw him lift off my skull and put it into my head? Is that what you saw?"

Ah, the signs of congenital catastrophe. Miles was Sarah's son all right, and well enough she knew it. The difference was that she, being the mother, could stop a slide into absurdity, while her son, being a parental extremity, could not.

"Yes, I saw him lift off your skull and you did just what he said to do."

Sarah stared hard bull's-eyes at Miles and said directly through him to Hugh, "You see, Hugh, what I have to put up with? Have you ever heard such a thing? A son talking to his mother like that? And here someone killed poor Bryan. I just can't believe it."

The word cocked Hugh's ear. "Someone killed him, Sarah?"

She turned her dagger eyes from Miles, but she couldn't register the question fast enough.

Miles did it for her. "Murdered? He was murdered!"

She snapped back to him. "He was killed."

"What's the difference?"

Hugh drew her attention back with, "When did this happen?"

"Just now. They just found him."

"At his office?" Miles asked, eyes wide.

"Yes, if you must know."

Miles jumped to his feet and slapped Hugh's shoulder with the back of his hand. "Come on, let's get over there!"

"Miles, you sit down. Where do you think you're going?" said Sarah, her forefinger jackhammering his chair.

"Hugh, let's go," he said, his hands pleading. The agony of expectation curled his whole shivering body into a bent exclamation point.

"Miles, I don't think—"

"Let's get over there before it's too late."

"Miles! You're going no such place," Sarah said, snapping out the words. She was really saying, *Miles, you silly twelve-year-old.*

He grabbed Hugh's arm and pulled him to his feet. "He was murdered!"

By the time they were out the front door and onto the porch, Sarah had heaped a series of belittling descriptives on Miles, all of them referring to juveniles. By the time Miles dragged Hugh down the steps to his Audi, the epithets had changed to the ghoulish and exotic. Hugh was exempt. He was being dragged away by her baby-fat little boy. It wasn't Hugh's fault.

Miles opened the car door and said, revolving his arm, "Let's go, let's go!"

Hugh half hurried to the driver's side, then looked over the car roof to Sarah, standing crushed-shouldered on the porch. He lifted his arms in apology. Meanwhile, Miles sat in the passenger seat and bobbed his body for the car to get moving.

Sarah accepted the wrong man's good-byes and shouted at the departing car, "What about Amy?"

Nowhere in Boston could Miles Cooper sidle past a Cerberus officer at the door of a murder scene, but in Longfield he managed it nicely, mainly because no officer was stationed at the door and, besides, everyone knew everyone else. A fledgling police chief with an imported academy degree wasn't going to change anything much. The news spread like a crackling fire from one telephone to another, once the report was picked up by wives of the Rescue Squad listening to their husbands' scanners.

12

Longfield was, after all, a citizens' town, and citizens had more than a right to know what was going on. In fact, they had a duty to know.

Miles interpreted *his* duty as one requiring on-the-scene participation. An extraordinarily loud whistle announced his entrance to Bryan Sheehan's office. The chief and four Rescue Squad members turned to hear Miles continue with, "Wow! Look at that!"

They saw Hugh next to him and studied him.

The lawyer was slumped over his desk, angled like a stringless puppet, his hands limp and grotesque on the desktop. His head was twisted sideways to a position that no one alive would be able to imitate. His mouth was open, like a screamless Munch. His thin gray hair looked out of place, pressed tight to his head and well combed. What made this rather quiet scene jarring was not the eerie paralysis of the man or the relatively mild leftovers of the death—the office was far from disrupted. In fact, it was rurally benign, as a proper Longfield law office should be. What was jarring was the absolutely vertical line of the weapon stuck into Bryan's back and how it had swung up as Bryan plunged down. The weapon, a letter opener, had words on it that read: "Welcome to the White Mou . . ."

"He was murdered all right," Miles had to say aloud.

"Miles," said the chief in greeting. He'd smile later, maybe. Then he looked at Hugh and waited for the introduction to find out who this was.

"You do it, Miles?" one of the men said, and the rest of the Rescue Squad grinned and laughed a little.

"I did something, Toop, but I didn't do that."

The only uniform there reached out for Hugh's hand. "I'm Chief Maddox," he said when Miles kept staring at the murdered lawyer.

"Oh, yeah," Miles said. "This is Hugh Quint. That's Chief Maddox, Toop Tucker, the other guys. Whatever."

"I live in Arcadia," Hugh said, reassuring the chief that,

13

yes, he lived in the same state at least; that, yes, he could talk without going quirky with a dead man in sight.

"Yeah, Chief," Miles said. "Hugh's a detective with the Boston police. He'll solve this for you. He does this all the time. You should see him work. Why don't you hire him? Go ahead, hire him or something. He's the best they got down there, does this stuff all the time." Miles snapped his fingers.

Oh, God.

"He does?" the chief asked.

"All the time," Miles said.

"Miles," Hugh said, "I think . . ."

"He *loves* to do this stuff. I mean, that's his job, that's what he does."

"Miles . . ."

"He's a specialist in murder stuff."

Chief Maddox nodded.

"He *is*."

Chief Maddox stood like a crisp young chief of police whose jurisdiction was enlarging at the speed of light from Longfield to infinity. The more Miles talked, the farther the chief's shoulders edged back, the more his mouth tightened, bristling his trimmed moustache up and out. No sign of a smile on him at all.

"I *was* with Boston," Hugh said, eyeing Miles.

"Whatever. He was a lieutenant, Chief. A detective on the homicide squad or something. Solved them all. Why don't you hire him?"

"Judas, Miles."

"What?"

"We'll keep you in mind," the Chief said.

"I work on my own now," Hugh said, which was all he needed to say.

But Miles had to say, "He's a private detective. Or is it private investigator? I don't know. Who cares? Wow! Old Bryan really got it. Who did it?"

14

The chief glanced at Hugh, who raised his eyebrow and twisted his mouth, something he did a lot around Miles. "We don't know yet." He turned back to Hugh.

"*Some*body did it," Miles said. "Look at that knife!"

"Yeah," the chief said.

"Got any clues?"

The chief ignored him.

"Who found him?" Hugh asked.

He followed the chief to the desk. Miles followed Hugh. The office had a lawyerly solemnity about it. The wainscoting that skirted the lower half of the wall was shiny mahogany. The upper half was painted ivory. A Seth Thomas clock ticked in the corner and swung in time, with its long polished panels of red rock maple and filigree minute and hour hands. The burgundy-colored carpet, wall-to-wall, quieted the office for serious concerns. Leather chairs, a round table large enough to seat four, steel-gray file cabinets, Early American anonymous portraits in gilded antique frames, a Childe Hassam print, and built-in bookcases completed the motif. Everything neat and trim.

The ten-inch-thick iron door to the walk-in vault was half open. It was a small safe, scarcely large enough for three file cabinets and room to use them. Nothing was piled on top of the cabinets. Neat and trim too. Except for the first drawer in the first cabinet, which had been left ajar, like the door.

"Cathy found him," the chief said. "It's her day off, but she came back to mail something, she says."

"She's Bryan's ol' secretary," Miles said, leaning around to make sure Hugh heard him.

"She left when we arrived," the chief said.

"You want me to get her, Chief?" Toop asked from the side. "Chances are she's back home."

The chief shook his head. "Leave her be."

"She's sort of funny, you know," Miles said to Hugh.

15

"You hear that, Chief?" Toop said. "Thomas Edison here says Cathy's kind of funny. Sounds to me like the kettle calling the pot nuts." The others laughed and called, "Yeah, what about that, Miles?"

Miles pointed to Toop and said to the chief, "If you're after clues about Toop, don't look for them, smell them."

They all laughed, and that was the end of that.

Up close, Hugh saw that Bryan's desk was as orderly as the rest of the office. A wooden file-in/file-out box had plenty of room for more papers and reports. He walked around to the other side. All the drawers were closed, except the bottom one, which could have sprung open with the impact of Bryan's head and shoulders on the desktop. Nothing was ransacked, nothing was out of place or unusual—it was the standard catchall drawer of sharpened pencils, boxes of paper clips, notepads, stapler, rulers, comb, deck of cards.

Bryan's pants appeared untouched, no pockets turned inside out from robbery. His jacket, on the hanger at the opposite side of the room from the clock, hung straight, with no sign of rifled pockets.

The law books were lined up in the built-in bookcase military perfect. A second panel of general reference books was equally in step, nothing out of sync.

"You up visiting?" the chief asked, trying to sound casual, though casual hardly ever exuded from flat-stomach officers with tight belts.

"Partly," Hugh said, "Amy hasn't been checking in lately and Sarah is a little concerned." He glanced at Miles, who wagged his head in mock self-castigation.

"She mentioned something like that," the chief said. Then he nodded toward the body and added, "But I've got to worry about this."

Hugh looked around the office. "This was an old bank, I take it," he said to change the subject.

"How'd you know?" Miles asked. "Sure, it used to be a bank in the old days and then a regular old house and then

16

Bryan took it for his office. How'd he know that?" He looked to the chief for confirmation that Hugh was an investigative genius and should be hired right away.

Hugh smiled. "It's on the door of the safe, Miles. 'The White Mountain Bank of Longfield.'"

Miles stepped to the door and read the gilt lettering, his head bobbing in amazement. "I told you he was good," he declared to the chief. "This man is *good*. Will you look at that?"

The chief nodded and twisted his mouth so that his head followed suit. "Yeah."

Hugh turned his back on the grinning crowd: "Judas, Miles." He finally caught the chief's eye. "Anything missing?"

"We don't know yet."

The answer was standard police academy response, what with the control center of the town peering at them and half the population likely to know what went on inside Bryan's office three minutes after the Rescue Squad left with the body.

"The state troopers'll be here," the chief said. "They'll try to find some latents and take some photos. Once I get all these guys cleared out of here."

The men grumbled.

"Come on, let's go," the chief said, scooting the men out. "The state'll crucify me if they see this crowd in here. Out, out."

"We're solving this," Miles said.

"Out."

They single-filed out, with Miles putting up the most argument. He lingered with Hugh as the last one out. Hugh stopped to say something to the chief while Miles leaned around with his upturned eyes and rapt attention.

"You might have Cathy check that first file," he said to the chief. "There might be something in that one that's missing. It looks like the only one that's been opened."

The chief looked into the safe and nodded.

"You see, Chief," Miles said, "you see. Will you look at that? I mean, he is something. Hire him. Why don't you *hire* him?"

Oh, Judas, Miles.

18

3

BETWIXT THE DEVIL AND THE DEEP SEA.
—ERASMUS

WHEN SARAH HAD finally assembled the two wayward men at her dining-room table again, she folded her presiding hands in her lap and said with regal rectitude, "Shame on you grown men traipsing after tragedy like that."

Hugh and Miles sat silent for their punishment. They had, after all, abandoned her for a race against rigor mortis, a shameful, ambulance-chasing act in itself, let alone the abandonment. They deserved this scourge.

But for Miles the one-minute sentence and punishment had gone on long enough. "I was trying to get Hugh a job," he said, Clarence Darrow to the rescue.

"You were not," she said, forming each word like rolled biscuits, and in no hurry.

"I was."

She turned to Hugh. "Was he trying to get you a job?" she asked with the obvious implication that Miles Cooper didn't know what a job was in the first place.

"To tell you the truth, Sarah," Hugh said, "I thought he was trying not to get me a job."

Miles supplicated heaven. "Can you believe it? Here I am hustling a job for him, doing his dirty work, and he says I'm a dodo bird."

"I didn't say that."

"Sure you did."

"Well, *I'm* saying it," Sarah said. "You are a dodo bird."

19

Miles deflated himself with a disgusted, kicked-dog look and turned away.

"Poor Bryan," she said. "I just can't believe it. Who would do such a thing? But I don't want to hear what you saw."

"I know," Hugh said. "Tell me about Amy."

Her eyes softened. She fell silent and stared at Hugh across from her. She saw the sandy-haired, high-cheek-boned savior who would find Amy for her—the man who knew the difference between Claude Lévi-Strauss and the blue jeans, even if she didn't know. He was the tall and lean detective with a Back Bay air about him. He knew what to do. He would help her. He was kind. She could count on him—unlike her very own son. Hugh had been a classmate of her son, only he had made something of himself on the Boston police force, and he had old Boston family heritage. So what if he couldn't take orders for long and had to go on his own? That was all right, because then he could help her when she needed him. Like now. Some men just had to go on their own, that's all, nothing wrong with that. Being a private detective was a good job. And he didn't even need to do that, with that family background and all. He liked to live away from Boston, and he wasn't trying to do all these schemes and everything. Why wasn't he her son? He was looking at her with all his might and wanted to help her. He even read books too.

She reached over and patted his hand. "Hugh dear."

"What makes you so worried about her?"

"It's that Eric boy. I think she's with him, and I wish she would just settle down and think about Calvin. He likes her so much, Calvin does. Why doesn't she like him back?"

Miles had to say it: "I know why. Anybody knows why."

"You just don't like any of the Tuckers, and I know why too."

"Well, what do you expect, Mother? Besides, Amy is old enough to take care of herself."

20

"I'm talking to Hugh, not you. I'm telling him about Amy. You wouldn't tell him about her, would you? I know you, Miles Cooper."

"Tell him about her then," he said, and sniffed defeat again.

Sarah paused for composure, inhaled, and said, "Now Hugh dear, you know Amy is adopted and she has some Abenaki in her, and now I think she's been seeing a lot of this Eric Fielding."

Miles turned straight in his chair again. "Eric *Cornplanter*," he said. "Eric *Cornplanter*. He changed his name, Mother. That's his name. Everybody knows it."

"I don't know it," she said and watched Miles flip his hand in abject response.

Hugh turned the tide with, "And you think Amy is with Eric someplace? Run away with him?"

"She's never been away so long."

"Three days," Miles said to the wall.

"Four days. And I ought to know."

"She's of age, Sarah," Hugh said gently.

"It's not right for her. Something wrong will come of it. I'm sure of it."

Hugh smiled and nodded. "I'll check into it," he said to the woman who had plied him with noon soup and apple pie. Could he say anything else?

She brightened with thanksgiving. "Will you, Hugh dear?"

"I'll see what I can find out. There's probably nothing to worry about."

"You'll find her, won't you?"

"I'll try."

She smiled and sighed. "Now you just plan on staying here with us," she said. "We have a nice room for you and I'll fix you food that you need, Hugh dear. I know what you need. So you just do that."

Hugh held up his hands. "Sarah, I'd rather get a separate place while I'm up here."

21

"I won't hear of such a thing."

"I think I should. I work better that way."

"I never heard of such a thing. You'll stay here."

Miles squirmed in his chair.

"Really," Hugh said.

"I know what you need, Hugh dear, so you stay here."

"Mother," Miles blurted, "he wants to stay someplace else."

"He does not."

"He does too. Did you hear him? He said, 'I want to stay someplace else.' That's what he said."

"He never said any such thing, Miles Cooper."

Miles twisted the other way in his chair. "Are we through here or what?"

"It's better that way," Hugh said, nodding. "I'll find a motel someplace on the highway."

Sarah frowned acquiescence.

"Are we through here or what?" Miles repeated.

"Oh, *Miles*!"

"All I asked was a simple question."

"You won't be staying at any such motel," Sarah said. She pursed her lips. "I'll call Jean. She has a guest cottage or two out back."

Miles inhaled loud and clear. "Call Jean. Are we through?"

Sarah steadied her gaze on the chubby-faced fiend and enunciated, "Yes, we are through."

"Good," Miles said and jumped to his feet. "Come on, Hugh. I'll show you what I've got going. You'll love it, it's fantastic. This is the one, all right."

Sarah shook her head. "I knew it."

Hugh grinned a mutual understanding of the inevitable and stood up.

"I'll call Jean and let you know, Hugh dear."

"Call Jean," Miles said. "Come on, Hugh, let's go."

"Then I'm going to call the devil after you, Miles

Cooper, and you can be sure of that, you bad boy!"

The barn was a clutter of contraptions, parts and pieces and junk and helter-skelter debris. Miles booted a copper tube out of the way and hurried Hugh to the worktable in the center of the mess. Piping, C-clamps, soldering irons, propane tanks, hammers, sheet metal, sledgehammers, hacksaws, test tubes, Bunsen burners, rolls of paper, rags, electrical cords, open brandless cans of white and gray and red powder, barrels of waste metals—on and on it went. The place was a colossal dump.

He shoved a jar of tar away. "See this," he said. "What do you think it is?"

Hugh shrugged. "It's a battery."

"Ha! This isn't just a battery. This is what I called you about. This is the *future*! This is IT!"

Hugh stared at the twelve-volt battery and waited.

"What is driving the world to death? What is killing the modern world? What's pitting the East against the West? Come on, what? It's the essence of the twentieth century, it's causing the whole world to go into debt, it's the ruination of civilization. What, what?"

Hugh shrugged. "I don't know, Miles. Batteries?"

"Energy! What uses energy like water every day, like it's going out of style? What, what?"

Hugh shrugged. "What?"

"Cars!" Miles said, sputtering, his hands clawing at the concept. "This is going to revolutionize cars. Electric cars! This is what's going to do it. I've got this fantastic electric battery powerful enough to run cars. Don't you see?"

"They've invented electric cars already, Miles."

"I know they've invented electric cars, but the batteries are too big. This is a sodium-sulfur battery reduced to only three times the size of ordinary twelve-volt lead oxide batteries and—this is it—powerful enough to run a car. That's always been the hangup. They couldn't get the size down enough. They couldn't get it small enough to fit into a car and have room left over and still be powerful enough to run it. I did it!"

Hugh looked back and forth from Miles to the battery. "That's great."

"I know it!"

"And you've tested it?"

"I'm testing it. This is high tech. This isn't your ordinary venetian-blind mop, you know. And that's the thing. I need more equipment, test meters, things like that." He held up a flat thumb and forefinger an inch away. "It's that close to revolutionizing the world, not just Main Street down there, the whole *world*. You want to get in on this on the ground floor? Now's the time!"

Hugh pursed his lips and grinned.

"They laughed at the electric light bulb *before* the fact. Who laughs now? Nobody!"

"You're into high tech, Miles."

"I know, I just told you, but I'm really into the future. Right now I need a few thousand to get there, and you can join up. What do you think?"

"You need a laboratory at G.E., Miles."

"I just need a few thousand dollars and we're all set. I'd sell that old chest if I could, but there's that stupid will of hers."

"You mean that grand old high chest of Sarah's? The Dunlap? She'd never forgive you."

"I couldn't anyway, not if I want to stay alive. Old Bryan made sure of that, the old fart lawyer."

"How's that?"

"He got Mother to make that will, that's how. It's stupid. He *made* her do it. You know what he did? He made her put in her will that when she dies Amy gets the chest and I get the house. The *full*-blooded Cooper line is supposed to stay intact with me and the house. So do you think I can sell the house when I want to? Hell, no."

24

"Why not?"

"Because when Daddy died, old bonehead Bryan made Mother fix up what Daddy left her, which means the house, of course, and the high chest. He made her put in the will that Amy could store the high chest in the house and have domicile privileges as long as she keeps the chest there. In fact—can you believe this?—the will says that if Mother dies and I try to sell the thing, I can't. I can't sell it if Amy still wants to store the chest in the house. It's stupid and *weird*."

"What does Amy think about it?"

"Who knows? She's out with Eric Cornplanter or something, planting corn, how do I know?"

"Sarah must have had some reason for that," Hugh said, suspecting what it was already.

"Who knows? I don't. Oh, something about how she wants to make sure that Amy *always* has a place to come back to. 'A roof over her head,' she says. She thinks I'm going to do something crazy like sell the house or something. So I can't do it if Amy keep that damn chest. The *chest* always has a place to stay—my house!"

"Which really means Amy does."

"Well, how am I going to have a roof over *my* head if I don't have enough money to keep inventing stuff to *have* a roof over my head, tell me that, will you, go ahead."

"Sounds to me like you both have something."

"Not to me. The only thing that's worth anything is the house. That chest is just some old Dunlap thing. That dumb bunch of drawers is worse than a coffin. It's *strangling* me, it's tying up the house, and I can't do anything with it."

"Miles, it's not yours yet, you know. Sarah is in good fiddle."

"Whatever. Besides, what does Amy want with a high chest anyway? I mean, what is she going to do with it? Store corn seed in it? What? If she sells it, she doesn't have a roof over her head. If she doesn't sell it, I don't have a roof over my head. Besides, maybe it's a roof I don't want. Mother says, 'It's something she can count on if she ever gets in trouble.' *I'm* the one that's got the trouble. You won't invest a few measly thousand in this revolutionary power source, and I sure don't see any revolutionary money source coming in down the road. *That's* the trouble. We're not talking mysticism here, we're talking money."

Hugh smiled as Miles stretched out his theatrical hands to underpin the profundity.

"You see my predicament?"

"I do."

"There ought to be a law against wills like that."

"Maybe she changed it and didn't tell you."

"And now someone sticks a pin in old Bryan's back. How's she going to change it?"

"Miles, there are other lawyers."

"Not for Mother there aren't. A few thousand, Hugh, a few measly thousand. You want immortality? This is your chance. I'll name it after you—The Hugh Quint Battery. Da da! Lights! Action! Fame! *Money*! Twenty or thirty thousand, that's all I need."

"Come on, Miles."

"Whatever."

Jean Gerard was less than Hugh had anticipated—God bless Sarah Cooper—and a lot more than he'd expected—God bless Longfield. She had auburn hair, and she knew it.

"You're Hugh Quint," she said before he could get his eyes off her hair and onto her bright blue eyes.

He smiled.

She smiled.

4

MEN ARE NOT HANGED FOR STEALING HORSES,
BUT THAT HORSES MAY NOT BE STOLEN.
— GEORGE SAVILE

BEFORE JEAN SWUNG the door back to invite him in, Hugh had already been distracted to little boyishness. It was her creamy highlander skin, so perfect with the auburn hair, that did it.

He couldn't have been more than a month beyond the dawn of reason and certainly light years before opening a dictionary when his father told him that their family name, Quint, meant "fifth." Burst of Helen Keller insight upon his young heart: names actually meant something, as if he, and everyone else with a name, meant something. If his last name had meaning, so must his first.

"Let's see," his father had said, glint in his omniscient eye. "It means 'mind.' That's why we picked it."

What were fathers for but to presume our greatness. For days young Hugh called himself Mind Fifth, which contained a lot more mystery than meaning. Finally, he settled into plain Hugh Quint for its sociability and ease, but most of all for its comprehensibility.

As he grew older, he broke the ice with shy, beautiful girls by delineating the derivations of their names—girls who, *he* was certain, considered him a whiz kid, but who no doubt regarded him as someone not to be trusted with much more than their names. Fortunately, beautiful girls bloomed into women, and now, as surely as youthful

27

bluster turned to mellow routine, Hugh stood in the center of the cozy gray-stained pine front room with sleek-boned Jean Gerard. She wore an open, blue, flap-tailed shirt over a Black Forest green turtleneck and butter-colored kick-around pants.

"Gerard, you probably already know," he said, "comes from someone who is particularly strong with a spear, but the Jean is a little more involved."

She kept on smiling, the old trooper, but her eyes showed hesitation. *This is the first thing he says?*

Suddenly, Hugh saw himself stumbling like an adolescent giraffe toward the precipice. What the hell was he doing? "Bad form," he said, shaking his head, grinning, retreating.

"I'm Hugh Quint, right, and you're Jean Gerard. Sarah said you might have a cottage for me."

"Yes, I do," she said, her eyes on him, maybe liking him. Who could tell?

What an idiot. "Did I see them out back?"

"Yes. Right out back. Sarah said you were a friend of the family."

"Oh, yes, I went to school with Miles."

She smiled.

"What's the matter?"

"Well, it's just refreshing to hear that."

He didn't understand.

"That you didn't say you went to Harvard."

"I'm afraid I did."

"I know. Because Miles did. Usually everybody who goes to Harvard lets everyone else know as soon as possible."

Hugh shrugged. "It's overrated. A school's ego is as big as its endowment."

She laughed. "Well, are you going to tell me or not?"

Ah, she forgives. Her eyes match her shirt. Her sleeves are rolled to mid-forearm: she's working. Sarah said she was an artist. Her hair is barretted back on both sides, efficiently

28

elegant, elegantly efficient. She is bright-eyed and bright-faced. Rounded jaws, soft nose. No flinty edges to her.

"You mean the Jean business?"

"You're not going to leave me in the lurch after all that, are you?"

"What can I say? Well, first of all, Jean is a very pretty name."

She smiled. *She* knew when to stop.

"Anyway, originally, it was the French form of John. Plus the letters J-e-a-n are the same letters as Jane. It's a simple rearrangement. Then from there, it evolved into Joan. Who knows why? Maybe people were slurring the sounds and a letter was changed when it was written. Joan is a form of Johanna, which you can tell by the way it sounds. And Johanna is the feminine for John. So there you go."

Her eyes on him were fixed hard, maybe to hear what he was saying, or maybe she was looking at him more than hearing him.

"Very impressive," she said, nodding, grinning.

He waved his hand in imperial nonchalance. He had, in fact, gone through the Jean scheme some five or six times before. Young boy impressionable ferments into young man impressing.

"I know you're a detective too," she said.

"Private investigator. Onetime gumshoe."

Now that was interesting. This woman wasn't going to ask about the obvious absurdity of a Harvard philosopher transmogrified into a back-alley P.I. Probably it was Sarah who told her that Hugh came from a Back Bay family of jewelers, textile importers, champagne merchants, and sundry enterprises of that ilk. Dear Hugh was just an aberration of the family who took his ancient Greeks seriously, and look what happened. But he was a good boy at heart, and Sarah just wished that now that he was no longer with the Boston Police Department he would prove himself in another field besides missing persons and murderers.

"Sarah said you're going to find Amy. I know she's worried about her."

"Has Amy done this before?"

"She disappears in the mountains for awhile, a few days, and then she comes back and everything's all right. It's just a phase. She's trying to find herself and deciding what to do with her life. She lives at home and so Sarah feels responsible for her. Any mother would."

"Of course. Do you know somebody named Eric Cornplanter?"

She smiled. "Yes. He's an interesting one, and I think Amy is smitten by him. But he's pretty elusive. Nobody sees too much of him, but then everybody knows about him, and talks about him, of course. He's a full-blooded Abenaki, they say. He lives in the mountains someplace, although nobody seems to know where exactly. I wouldn't be surprised if she's there with him. Do you know Amy?"

"I haven't seen her in years."

"She's a grown woman. You probably wouldn't recognize her."

"Time marches on. And Calvin Tucker?"

"Calvin Tucker. What can I say about Calvin Tucker? He's the son of Toop Tucker. He grew up with Amy. They were the best of friends. They were always together, until Eric showed up. Calvin works with his father lumbering. They're roughhewn, solid stock, like the work they do. Sarah always figured that Calvin and Amy would settle together, have a family."

"What do you think?"

"A young woman might smooth out the edges on Calvin, polish him up and bring him out a little. Maybe Amy is the one. I don't want to say."

"Maybe not."

She shrugged. "I'll tell you where the Tuckers live, if you want to talk with Calvin."

"Good, thanks. He might have seen Amy."

"You should talk with Asa Nickerson too. He knows this country like the palm of his hand. He's a loner. I'll draw you a map to his place. It's kind of complicated. He knows what's going on, more than he lets on too." She paused. "Isn't that terrible about what happened to Bryan?"

It was, he told her, and then asked if the painting over the mantel and the three on the walls were hers. Yes, she said. They were filled with the rich earth colors of the tall grass surrounding Longfield, and the White Mountains with their ocher-granite edges and tops, thick forests and flat-bottomed, sun-enameled rivers. The scenes had the obliqueness of human creation, not camera copying. They were more than what they depicted.

She showed him the cottage, told him to dial one to get an outside line on the phone, and drew him maps to the Tuckers' home and Asa Nickerson's place. The cottage held two chairs, refrigerator, stove, maple drop-leaf table, double bed, two of her own paintings. Clean as a whistle.

He thanked her and resisted the urge to expound on Sarah Cooper's last name, which stemmed from coop or enclosure. A cooper was one who made barrels in a cooperage, the place where a cooper worked. Easy. Well, let it go.

She said she'd see him later. He agreed. She smiled over her shoulder and walked through the scattered pines to her home. He watched her plenty. She knew it.

The Tucker farmhouse had settled on the north end so that the illusion of its clapboard lines tilted the house more than the inches it had sunk. Out front lay a pile of fieldstone ready for repairing something or building something. A stack of brush to the right blocked a trodden path that was weed ragged on its edges. The paint on the house was flaking on the left side of the door. On the right side someone had scraped the clapboard for repainting, but that was some time ago.

31

Tractors, haulers, chainsaws, thick chains, spare truck tires, shovels, and rope were strewn near the barn-garage. Black ground where oil dribbled from engine blocks spotted the gravel-and-sand driveway far beyond what anyone would consider decent. A red, rusted truck fender leaned against the side of the garage.

A birdbath stood directly in front of the main door with grass half a foot high around its base. It was half filled, although the bottom was smudgy dark with moss and algae. Golden retrievers would favor it more than blue jays.

Zeta opened the door as Hugh walked past the garage. He'd made it halfway to the house before Toop opened the side door of the barn to see who it was. Hugh was caught in the middle. He turned to Zeta, then regretted it. Toop had been with the Rescue Squad at Bryan's office, good for some introductory link.

Zeta stood in the red-splotched farmhouse doorway, her yellow flower print dress frumpy at the waist and askew at the hem. Her brown sweater was fastened with the two buttons at the bottom. She waited for Hugh to say something.

"Mrs. Tucker?"

"That's me," she said, stepping to the foot-gouged granite slab that old houses use for steps.

Hugh turned around. "You're Toop, I think. You were at Bryan's yesterday."

"Yep, I recognize you. You were with that wacko Miles. Sure I seen you there," Toop said, stepping closer. "He got it, all right. In the back, square on. Old Sheehan. Who are you again?"

"Hugh Quint. I'm a friend of Sarah Cooper."

Zeta called out: "I can't hear you from there!"

"Just hold on, woman," Toop shouted back and walked with Hugh toward her. "He's a friend of Sarah's."

She nodded and said, "Oh, yes, Mrs. Proper." Then she rubbed her right elbow.

Hugh let it go. It was their territory.

"Like I say," Toop said, grinning and grizzly, his maroon workshirt soiled with tree dirt and bark, gray heavy-duty pants misshapen with wear and tear, boots spotted and scuffed, "somebody had it in for old Sheehan. So you're detecting it. I heard it there, you know."

"No, I'm sure the chief can deal with it."

Toop laughed, arching his head back, a good belly laugh that made Hugh grin in return. He couldn't help it. "The chief? He's still wet behind the ears. Naw, he's still looking for last Friday. And two to one he ain't finding it neither."

Hugh smiled. The man had more in him than he'd thought. "No, I'm just checking around about Amy, that's all."

"Oh, you'll get in it, I suspect."

"She missing again?" Zeta asked, shaking her head and clicking her tongue. "Where she goes I'd like to know about. She's all right probably." She turned on Toop. "And don't you start laughing when somebody just got killed and murdered, Mr. Gambling Man."

"Don't start on me, woman."

She ignored him faster than an eye blink. "Now Amy's just gone someplace a while," she said right off, overlapping Toop's words. "Nothing wrong with that."

"Well, Sarah is a little worried about it."

"Mrs. Proper is always worried, young man," Zeta said, shaking her head with the sewing-needle eyes. "There's always something going on when there's nothing going on, if you understand what I'm saying. How close a friend are you?"

"Pretty long time."

"You ain't from here, I can tell that," she said. "There's a difference between knowing somebody a long time from afar and knowing somebody a long time up close. I knowed her a long time up close."

"True," Hugh said, nodding. And it was.

33

"Amy ain't been around here recently," Zeta said. "Has she, Toop?"

"Nope, but . . ."

"So you see, that's it."

Hugh nodded. "Maybe Calvin has seen her."

"Calvin ain't seen her," she said.

"Maybe he has," Toop said.

"Maybe he *hasn't*," she fired back, eyeing Toop, and then changing back quick to Hugh. "Calvin's in the woods working. He ain't seen her." She stared those needle eyes again at Hugh, evaluating. "You know, Mrs. Proper still got the Tucker high chest over there. Still got it."

"Dang blame it, woman!" Toop said like corn popping. "Don't start in on that again, I ain't listening to that, I ain't." He turned his back and hooked his thumbs in his front pockets. "It's through, and you got no call sticking on that like an old stuck record. Right in front of him too. What's the matter with you anyhow?"

"She still got it, you know, that Tucker high chest."

Hugh looked from one to the other. Toop was muttering with his back turned. "I don't quite understand."

"You got something to learn then, young man," Zeta said. "Something to learn right enough."

"Woman, leave it be."

"You go ask Mrs. Proper," Zeta told Hugh. "She'll tell you about it. Maybe she will, maybe she won't. Then *I'll* tell you about it. Because Mr. Gambling Man here sure ain't going to tell you. I know that enough."

Toop whirled around, face on fire, hot and hatchety.

"You don't scare me," Zeta said, "acting like that with this stranger guest coming to see you."

Toop stared at her until finally he loosened with the realization and glanced at Hugh watching him. "Leave it be," he said, quieter than the flame in his face.

"Well," Hugh said, stepping back, closing off, "I just thought you might know about Amy."

34

Why was he always in the crossfire? First between Sarah and Miles, now, Zeta and Toop.

"We don't know about Amy," Zeta said. A movement caught her eye and she turned. "There's Calvin now." She stared at him, mother spotting the dark nuances in son.

Hugh and Toop watched Calvin stride fast off the tote road to the driveway. His arms were swinging with purpose. He was half running, his face locked straight ahead, eyes tight set in small sockets like his mother's. His father showed in his wide shoulders and solid legs, blue jeans worn to white at the knees.

The three of them waited, mesmerized by his gait.

"Come on," Calvin said to Toop.

"What's wrong?" Zeta asked, the command in her voice softened by the disruption in Calvin's words and way.

"Come on," he repeated with the same alarming monotone. This time he looked at Hugh, the stranger. What was he doing there?

Toop stepped to him and bobbed his head back once in question.

"It's Danny."

They knew more was coming.

"He's hanging. Dead."

5

PROPERTY IS THEFT.

—PIERRE-JOSEPH PROUDHON

FINALLY, TOOP SAID, "Where?"

"Down by the old cellar hole."

Toop looked at Hugh with that sign of the male that said, Let's go together whether we know each other or not.

Calvin turned on his heel, the leader because he had found the hanging dead man. Hugh stepped out behind Toop, who shouted over his shoulder, "Call the chief."

"You ain't leaving me here," Zeta shouted back.

"Call the chief!"

"I'm coming with you," she countered.

"Women stay here. We're looking at a dead man out there. *Hanging* dead!"

"I knowed Danny when he was alive and I'm knowing him when he's dead," she said and reached inside the doorway for her boots. She squatted on the granite slab step, shoved her feet inside the boots, laced them up fast, and tromped after the three men striding down the driveway.

The four of them marched down the tote road through the thick woods, the three men now equalized in a line, Calvin marching on the ridge between the wheel ruts. Zeta matched their strides behind. Her boots fit, and her dress and sweater sort of fit. Together they made her the hefty-walking outback woman that she was.

They marched without a word. The way Calvin said "down by the cellar hole" sounded like over the next hill,

36

but on they walked through the blazing autumn maples and the late-turning oaks, the steady green pines and hemlocks. These were hardy folks used to the everyday outdoors, but Hugh was breathing hard and hearing himself do it. He had to get back in shape, all right. Long legs were only good for short walks if you were nothing but an unkempt bellows inside.

"Who is this Danny?"

"He lives around here," Toop said, and that was that.

They marched another fifteen minutes. Fifteen minutes without a word. Hugh wouldn't have imagined they could have kept quiet the whole time—not the way they'd been talking back at the farmhouse—but they did. They followed the tote road past a lumbered clearing, alongside the lake-black swamp with barkless trees standing like dinosaur leg stumps up and down the folds of the land. Then came the red swatch in the distance.

"There," Calvin said and pointed.

They walked past the cellar hole, the final remains of a long-gone backwoods farmhouse—a fieldstone foundation, one side caved in. The years had half spilled the land into the cellar and grown a weed cover with saplings squeezing against it.

The four of them stared up at the broken-necked corpse hanging like a dead flag. Danny Mayes. Maybe the same age as Toop and Zeta. He was wearing ordinary town shoes, tan corduroy pants, and a long-sleeved, blue-and-white-checked shirt. His neck was tied by two twisted red T-shirts, knotted together and then knotted around the hanging limb. White letters on the shirts were twisted undecipherably, but you could read them on one of the same red T-shirts that was pulled over his checked shirt. The white lettering arched across Danny Mayes's chest: "Welcome to the White Mountains."

At the farmhouse Zeta called the chief while Toop, Calvin, and Hugh waited out front beside the birdbath where the sun poured down. Calvin had the makings of the same taut skin and hefty frame that Toop possessed. His hair hung in black strands, without Toop's graying sideburns. He had the same big paw hands and feet. What Calvin didn't have of Toop was a quick, hot tongue and bluster. Here, Toop and Zeta flowed with the words. Out in the woods, they clammed up, as if the woods were their cathedral and you didn't blast out with a lot of blathering and yakking. You kept your mouth shut, because that was the way it had to be.

But the farmhouse—now that was where you mouthed off and talked your head off. That was where you did the blathering and shouting. Except for Calvin. He was as tight-lipped here as in the woods. Hugh had to see ahead whether that was just the way Calvin was, or whether some coals were smoldering inside.

"He didn't do that himself, you know," Toop said. "He got himself hanged up. Somebody did it for him, and I don't like it happening around here. Makes no sense and I ain't liking it. Something's going on here. You got to do some detecting around, you know."

Hugh saw the worried heat in his eyes. "He didn't have any reason to do it himself?" he asked, switching directions, seeing Calvin studying him.

"Hell, no," Toop said. "Nobody climbs up there and hangs himself with a tourist shirt on." He paused and stared at the unending stupidity of Boston-bred city dopes. "You put a tourist shirt on and execute yourself? Uh-uh, uh-uh. And too dang close to this place. I ain't liking it."

Zeta flung open the front door and shouted, "I called Mr. Law and Order." She clomped her boot-march down the granite slab and straight to the men.

"What'd you say to him?"

"I said Danny Mayes is hanging dead in a tree, and get yourself over here, and I hung up."

38

"That's all you told him?" Toop asked, sticking his neck out in disbelief.

"Yeah, that's all I told him."

"Well, why didn't you tell him something?"

"I told him what he needs to know."

"Well, why didn't you tell him how he's hanging? Did you tell him where?"

"In a tree."

Toop shoved a forefinger at the infinite woods. "A tree? A *tree*?"

"He's coming. I'll show him." She turned to Hugh. "He owns land around here and we log some. But now what? He goes and gets himself hanged. With that shirt on. What's that for?"

Toop cut in. "How could somebody do it?"

Hugh looked back and forth at them. "It looked like he was unconscious or killed first."

"How's that?"

"His head was gashed with something. Maybe that's when somebody put the shirt on."

"I didn't see that," Toop said.

"I did," Calvin said, glancing at Hugh.

Toop stared open-mouthed at his son.

"Why'd somebody put that touristy shirt on him anyway?" Zeta asked, needle eyes sewing into Hugh, holding him tighter than a zipper. "Some kind of murdering joke?"

"Murdering?" Toop said. "I don't like that."

"Sure it's murdering," she fired back at him. "Danny ain't suiciding himself with a red tourist shirt on. You can't see that, you can't see nothing."

"I know that."

"Well, show it."

Toop stared nails at Zeta, but it didn't do any good. She was already full of nails.

The chief drove up in his blue-and-white, parked it, got out flat-bellied and official, and walked over with his right arm swinging wide over his holster. The ambivalence in his tilted head betrayed the weak confidence he had in Zeta's one-line message. He believed her, all right, or he wouldn't have sped over. At the same time, Zeta's bluntness on the phone must have cast its share of doubt.

He nodded to everyone, a little slower on Hugh.

"I was over here asking about Amy," Hugh volunteered, "when Calvin told us about it."

The chief turned to Calvin, who stood firm and head-on. He had center stage, but it wasn't something he worked for, you could tell. He told the chief what he saw, when he saw it, and how they all went to see.

"Why didn't you call me first?" the chief asked Toop.

Zeta hurried in. "Because we had to see. He ain't going nowhere."

"You didn't touch anything," the chief said. It was a question he asked everyone as he looked to Hugh, who should have known better.

"No," Hugh said.

"He's hanging up the tree," Zeta said like a lesson in logic. How could they touch him?

The chief pursed his lips and nodded. "Let's go."

The Rescue Squad ambulance drove in. Everyone stopped to watch it ease up and squish pebble noises at them. The chief told the driver to follow them out the tote road where Calvin had pointed. The driver backed away so the chief could drive on first.

"He's been dead a while," Hugh said, stopping the chief and the others. "I think the medical examiner will show that."

"You seen a lot of hangings?" Zeta asked. "How come you know that?"

Hugh half shrugged.

"You want to show me, Calvin?" the chief asked, and Calvin stepped to the patrol car. Toop followed suit.

40

Zeta preempted the series. "I'm staying here. I seen it."

"Well," the chief said, "will you show the troopers where we are? They'll be coming."

"I'll tell them, Mr. Law and Order."

The chief stared at her a moment before moving to the car. Hugh stopped him with, "I was wondering. Did you ask Cathy if she found anything missing in that file?"

The chief paused, debating whether to tell him. "She did." Then he walked away from the car, away from Zeta, drawing Hugh along with him out of earshot of the others, who were watching. From training, he turned his back so they couldn't read his lips or catch the words on the wind.

This was a reward for spotting the open file drawer in the safe. Hugh gave the chief good marks when he heard him say, "It looks like Sarah Cooper's will is missing."

Better than he hoped. There was Jean Gerard out front raking leaves, black plastic catchall sheet to one side, patches of old green lawn cleared away to the other. Rust-colored scarf wrapping her auburn head. He turned into the driveway that ran past her cedar-shingled house to the cottages out back.

"You forgot that one over there," he called, leaning out the window, pointing to a lone leaf on the long grass.

She laughed and waved him quiet.

He turned off the ignition and got out. "I see you have only one rake."

"That's right," she said, holding it out. "You want to use it? This is great fun. I'll have to charge you a nickel."

"No, thank you, Becky Thatcher."

"I'm of two schools, actually," she said. "This year it's the rake-as-they-fall school. They tell me that spreads out the raking with a lot of little piles."

"Sort of like building a small campfire so you can get close to it instead of a big one and blazing yourself away from it."

"Well, sort of."

Hugh smiled. "That didn't make sense to me either."

"Last year I did the rake-after-they-all-fall trip. I waited until they were a foot thick and raked them all up at once. They say it saves time."

"Did it?"

"No. It gave me a sore arm and I couldn't paint for three days."

"What about next year?"

"I'm thinking of something new. I'm going to hire somebody."

He laughed, then said, "I've got a question."

"What's that?"

"What do you know about that high chest Sarah has in her front room?"

"It's a beauty, isn't it? An old Dunlap. Why?"

"I always thought it was in the family."

Jean stopped and shook her head. "You don't know the story on that?"

She told him that ten, maybe twelve years ago—she couldn't remember exactly—when Sarah's husband Eddie was alive, the story that first got out had later changed over the next few weeks but eventually straightened out. Apparently, Toop was in a poker game with Eddie and some others in town and the stakes got kind of high. A couple of times when the stakes got high, the men ran out of cash and they didn't want to drop out of the game. It was more exciting to bet something other than IOUs for cash. So they'd bet tools, like a plow or chainsaws, things like that. In some of the games they ended up betting land. Bryan Sheehan, in fact, lost two acres to Toop in one game. Then in the next game, or the next two—she couldn't remember which—he won them back. One time Bryan lost three acres to Toop and never did get them back.

Anyway, one game they were playing and, as usual, the stakes got high and Toop ran out of cash. He was always going around without enough money on him. Still does. It

42

was late at night and the playing was good and he didn't want to leave. The others were playing for high stakes and, well, you know how betting gets. It's an addiction. So Eddie, the story goes, had a good hand and was betting up the stakes. If Sarah had known at the time, she would have crowned his skull because in the end he was betting off ten acres down by the river in the back corner of their land where it was prize siting. He was that sure of his hand, or so he was playing it.

Meanwhile, Toop—who can hang in with the boys and bluff his way into anything—kept betting along with Eddie until they got into the last round and that piece of land of his. Eddie told Toop that Toop didn't have any land that matched his and he'd have to come up with something better than a boulder garden.

So Toop right away, the story goes, bet their high chest—their Dunlap. He said that was more than worth the Cooper land and it didn't matter because he said Eddie was bluffing and he had a hand that would take him. Only it was Toop that was bluffing in the end. He didn't even show his hand, and Eddie won the chest on a straight flush, king high.

It absolutely killed Zeta, and she practically killed Toop for it. He said the chest came with his family and he could do with it what he wanted. Ever since, Zeta has hounded Toop because of that, and that's the reason some bad blood runs between the Tuckers and the Coopers. In fact, Zeta keeps saying, after all these years, that Sarah has the "Tucker" high chest. She won't admit the transfer after all these years.

Sarah at first told Eddie to give it back, but Eddie said it was a man's game and a man had to stick to his word and honor. He'd put up some of his own Cooper land against it and would have had to give that up if he'd lost, but he didn't lose. So he said it was fair play, and Toop brought it on himself. He didn't have to bet the high chest, and he didn't have to keep bluffing the way he does.

"Besides that," Jean continued," Zeta keeps after Calvin and never lets him forget that his father lost that high chest in a poker game. That's not good for a boy like that to hear all the time. Well, he's not a boy anymore. Still . . .

"Anyway, the whole town knows about it. A lot of talk was going on when it first happened. Of course, Toop couldn't back out because the other players were there and heard it all. Then when Eddie died a few years later, that more or less settled it. Nobody could blame Sarah for keeping the chest with Eddie gone—except Zeta, of course. So that's how it went."

"Was Danny Mayes one of the players?" Hugh asked.

"He was. How did you know?"

6

YOU KNOW THE CAUSE OF OUR MAKING WAR. IT IS KNOWN TO
ALL WHITE MEN. THEY OUGHT TO BE ASHAMED OF IT.
—BLACK HAWK

ANY KIND OF detective work, police or private, was ninety-five percent information, five percent legwork. So Hugh stretched his legs onto a table and telephoned Proctor Hammond, his answerman.

"Quint."

"Oh."

"Such joy, Proctor. I'm overwhelmed."

"You always call when I'm doing something. You're the one who calls. I'm the one who does something."

"Finishing up the Unified Field Theory, huh?"

"Funny man in the funny woods in funny little Arcadia."

"Longfield. Why don't you take a little vacation north, Proctor? Get out of the city. Breathe a little oxygen."

"I prefer carbon monoxide, thank you very much. Not to mention the symphony, and the Fine Arts Museum, and the Shubert Theatre, and the Science Museum, and Steve's Greek Restaurant—"

"Right, Proctor."

"and Fenway Park, and Victor Hugo's Bookstore, and the Boston Common—"

"Right, right."

"and Quincy Market and the North End. I think you get my point."

"I get your point," Hugh said, grinning, listening to the

man's high chirpy voice, picturing him barricaded behind piles of gray archival storage boxes in the Special Collections section of the Mugar Library, Boston University. What else could he be but an archivist?

"You're such an urban creature, Proctor, with all those urban-grown tics."

"My tics are not the blood-sucking red monster ticks you farm up there in the northern Amazon, Quint, burrowing their heads into your thick hide and lapping up your wayward blood until you feel them killing you. Then you rip them off with your hand. But only their bodies come off because their heads are still buried in your hide where they rot, if they're not gobbling up more of your blood by left-over autonomic response. Then the rot turns to infectious poison and you're on your way to the grave while your tick is ticking away in tick heaven. It happened to me—once. And you recommend the great outdoors."

"You forgot the scary owls and other things that go bump in the night. *Treasure Island* must have scared you to death."

"What scares me to death is talking with you."

"I don't know why."

"Because you remind me of what the bucolic myth does to urban intelligence, of how perfectly normal city people turn into clodhoppers on the central common. These are the people who sneak up there to your mythic environs and steal gravestones from little old cemeteries. Then they bring them back here to Newbury Street and sell them to other oxygen-starved urbans for coffee tables. They call them flat sculpture. I call them flatheads. This wouldn't happen if New Hampshire didn't exist."

"You're such a charmer, Proctor."

"I know. Nobody goes to Longfield without an ulterior motive. Nobody has even heard of Longfield."

"Have you heard of Dunlap?"

"Dunlap tires, sure."

"No, not tires. I'm talking about high chests. Highboys."

"I'm talking about Dunlap tires. Second grade and cheap. Made in Communist Romania by Romanians at Communist wages and sold in this country at capitalist prices to confuse illiterate Americans—twenty-six million Americans can't read, you know—who think they're buying the Dunlop tires that everybody knows and admires and loves and respects. Twenty-six million Americans can't read the Bill of Rights or the label on a laxative bottle and you ask me about Communist tires."

"I'm asking you about Dunlap high chests made two hundred years ago."

"Twenty-six million Americans can't read a map let alone a newspaper or a checkbook or the Yellow Pages. They can't read an historical marker on the highway or what the bottle of bleach says. They brush their teeth with bleach because if it cleans their sheets so white it cleans their teeth too. Whiter than white, until they dissolve. That's what you're dealing with, Quint. That's why they don't know anything about the history of science because they can't *read* the history of science. They can't read—period."

"What are you working in a library for then?"

"Of course, I know Dunlap high chests. John and Samuel Dunlap made them from around seventeen seventy-five on. They were brothers and they made them in Bedford, New Hampshire, someplace. Then their sons made them, and now those chests are part of what is called the Dunlap School."

"You just looked that up, didn't you?"

"I read, Quint, I read. A fact here, a fact there, and pretty soon you have a million of them. Try it sometime."

"The more relationships you know, the less facts you have to know."

"We all see the philosopher in you, Quint, but a fact in the hand is worth two philosophers in the bush."

47

"You are a fund, Proctor. How much are these Dunlaps worth today?"

"It depends. If they have snakeskin notched knees, rosette capitals, claw-and-ball feet, you're off to a good start. It depends on the work, whether it has a five-tier upper case, four-drawer lower case. Maybe it has a basket weave on the cornice, maybe molded S-scrolls on the skirt. They all add up. It depends on the grain of the maple and how the wood is placed and preserved, how it's polished. It depends on the construction of the drawers themselves, how they fit and slide in and out, how aesthetically the different sizes of the drawers are graduated, whether the piece has any secret drawers. Secret drawers and secret compartments add public value, and the Dunlaps had their share of them. It depends on whether the chest was remodeled, whether the style was changed and turned into a disgusting mosaic. It depends. I think you get my point."

"Very impressive. So what's the *one* thing to look for in a Dunlap."

"That's easy. A signature. The Dunlaps made hundreds of furniture pieces. They were cabinetmakers, they did it for a living, they kept making them and they kept making them better."

"Why a signature then, if they made so many?"

"Because, Quint, of the *facts*. The fact is that the Dunlaps and their shop made hundreds of these chests and their account books show it. We have the account books, but we don't have their signatures. Not many anyway. They signed a few. Get an authentic Dunlap high chest that's signed and you've hit the jackpot."

"How much of a jackpot?"

"For somebody who really wants it—thirty-thousand dollars and up."

Hugh thought about it.

"I got your attention."

"How far up?"

"I've seen signed Dunlaps go for a hundred thousand dollars. But they have to be in top condition."

"This one is in prime shape. Maybe mint shape. Where do you find a signature?"

"Take out the drawers and look on the back inside panel. Or just look on the back outside panel. If there's one, it's probably chalked on. Maybe inked."

"*Chalked* on?"

"That's what they did."

"What if it's forged?"

"Those who know, know. And even those get greedy."

"Who knows?"

"Try James Johnson in Dedham, or Wendall Kellor in Wellesley."

"Thanks, fact man."

"Go get some more ticks. You're buying a high chest, I take it."

"No, a friend has a Dunlap. And I ran into some killings up here."

"Careful, Quint. Al Capone did the same thing and look where it got him. These killings are connected with the high chest, I take it."

"Maybe. Two women want one chest."

"So said Zeus."

"What?"

" 'Women and murder will kill you in the end.' "

Hugh followed Jean's map to Asa Nickerson's place. The back roads got narrower with each junction and turn. He cruised by the stepping-stone rivers and brooks, turned past a family plot cemetery fenced in with wrought iron, then headed straight for a quarter mile until he came to the Y-junction, where she had told him to go right for another quarter mile.

You can't miss it, she'd said. Turn in at the only gap in the trees. If you end up three-tenths of a mile from the junction, you've gone too far. Park your car and walk the trail. You'll find him. Or he'll find you.

He hiked up the trail and along a clearing that thrust the White Mountains into view. It was spectacular. The Presidential Range with its high rocky bald peaks cut the horizon, and the strength of the terrain, squat and muscular, kept him staring.

A crow cawed, and he walked on. Up the way a chickadee flitted alongside him, sounding its high dainty pitterpatter.

The pine-board cabin was snug against an upcrop of White Mountain to the rear. The front pointed straight to the sweeping horizon that Hugh had seen earlier. The cabin roof extended over the porch with one chair facing the edge of the universe.

"Asa?"

No answer. Hugh called again and then stepped onto the porch. Nobody stirred inside. He walked to the right side of the porch, looking in the windows as he went, then leaned over the log railing. Nobody around back.

"Asa?"

He walked back across the plank-wood porch to the other side. Nobody.

Well, obviously the man had no telephone, so how could Hugh have called beforehand? The place wasn't abandoned: it was too swept and tidy for that. The glass was clean. And Asa wasn't a note-leaver.

Hugh turned and looked at the clearing in front of the cabin. The ground was covered with needles, and it was impossible to trace any footsteps. The pine branches were clipped low, he could see that, probably to get headbleeders out of the way. He turned to the front window again, thinking of the Bible: "In the beginning was the guilt."

He stepped to the window and peered in. This place was lived-in, all right—a bowl in the sink, a book on the table in

50

front of the stovewood pile, the clock on the half-empty bookshelf that read about the right time.

He heard the same cawing of the crow. Only it was closer. Behind him. Ground level. The old guy was leaning against the fat-trunk hemlock to the right across the clearing, smiling and watching, and finally revealing himself. "Caw. Caw. Caw."

Hugh grinned. And shook his head at himself.

"Just seeing what you'd do up there," the old guy said, his voice chuckling more than the words said. "Just seeing whether you could tell the real thing or not."

He kept leaning against the tree, but his stance meant woodsman. Straight and alert, eyes taking it all in.

"You're Asa," Hugh said, nodding, answering his own question, being sure. He stepped from the porch.

"Chickadee-dee-dee. Chickadee-dee-dee."

Hugh laughed again. "That was you?"

Asa just stood there grinning.

Hugh took some more steps. "Jean Gerard mentioned you and said you might be able to help."

Asa nodded. "I know her."

This was no time to coy around. One didn't high-nose it in the woods with someone who lived with the raw basics and knew the difference between craft and candor, especially in his own woods.

"Actually, she thought you might be able to help me with finding Amy Cooper."

"Maybe so. I know Amy."

"Sarah's worried about her."

Asa nodded and stepped halfway to Hugh.

He thought he better say it. "I'm a detective."

"I know."

Hugh smiled and nodded. Of course, he'd better say it. Who didn't know it around here? "Maybe Eric Cornplanter might know where she is."

"Maybe."

51

"You know him," Hugh said midway between question and statement. Of course, Asa knew him.

Asa nodded.

"Do you know where I can find him?"

Asa grinned, old tough eyes playing dice with the young 'un. "Eric might be over there," he said, pointing to the far horizon through the clearing. "Or there"—to the left—"or there"—behind the cabin.

Up close Asa Nickerson was shorter than he looked from a distance. The green woolen shirt was a start on the cold autumn nights. His boots were molded to his feet, and they stood flat square on the ground facing Hugh. His black sheep-wool twill pants had built-in creases from walking the miles.

"You could ask Crow," Asa said. "Crow knows. Deer too. We got some fishers around here now, they're coming back, but I'd bank on Crow and Hawk. Golden Eagle knows a lot. They know Eric. They'll tell you."

"Good idea."

"I talk to them all, except Deer. They don't talk much back, but I know where they are. We get along."

"Next time," Hugh said, "ask them, will you?"

Asa grinned. "Eric is around."

"And Amy?"

"Trouble is," Asa continued, ignoring the question, "most white people don't know how to talk with Crow and Hawk. Eric is teaching me. So I guess that tells you something, doesn't it?"

Hugh nodded.

"These mountains are his, you know. We whites are just passing through, getting all we can while the getting's ripe. I used to do the same."

Hugh paused and let the man study him.

"Crow tells me that white people are eating the mountains. I tell Crow I know this. I've seen them hack the mountains for logging, hack it down for ski trails and fan-

52

tasy lands and merry-go-rounds. Crow asks what right do these people have to do that. Eric talks with Crow too."

The balance of Asa's eyes with his words kept Hugh listening. He didn't see any flight in the man's face.

"Amy's all right?" he asked, sensing it was true and Asa knew it.

"You have to know something about Eric. He's his people, and his people were this country, these mountains. They talked to Crow. They aren't here much, but he's here. You have to know that. He's in the wilderness. He's talking to Crow and Hawk and Beaver. He knows. He knows what to do."

7

VIOLENCE DOES NOT AND CANNOT EXIST BY ITSELF; IT IS
INVARIABLY INTERTWINED WITH THE LIE.
—ALEKSANDR SOLZHENITSYN

WHEN HUGH RETURNED to his cottage that night, the door was slightly ajar, enough for a sliver of moonlight to show through. The meaning of it didn't register at first. He was slow on the draw, detoured. He had finished dinner at Sarah's, spent two hours afterward thrashing over outlandish contraptions-to-come with Miles, and another hour trying to tear himself away from Miles's plea for a loan.

So Hugh was exhausted. Driving past Jean's house he'd seen the only light on in the back room—no doubt her bedroom. She was probably reading in bed. He diverted his attention to that sweet prospect.

He stared at the door until it registered that he well knew he had closed and locked it. He remembered checking the door, twisting the handle, and pushing the door to hear it clank against the lock. The door *was* locked, and a door did not unlock itself.

He stepped five feet in front of it and listened.

He remembered his grandmother's finger-wagging warning: curiosity killed the cat. She uttered it regularly from the first time Hugh steam-burned his little hand trying to peek under the lid of her simmering vegetable soup, the old-time good kind. Later his mother told him that once his grandmother had led her to the top of the cellar stairs and said, with a bony point of her hooked hand to

54

the dark below, "There's a dead man buried at the bottom of the stairs so don't ever go down there without me. Curiosity killed the cat." What the warning had to do with the dead man buried at the bottom of the stairs—and, naturally, there wasn't—Hugh never unraveled, but at the time and for decades to come, it worked. He grew up with a mother who was scared to death of dark cellars and dead people—not an altogether unique fear. And his grandmother had seared the dynamite lesson into his brain with her sorceress face and candied voice.

He heard nothing.

He could see nothing move either. He gave it another thirty seconds, a cautious eternity in the woodsy night. Why was he now the intruder in his own place?

Wait a little more, he told himself, and he did. Doors don't speak, and neither do cottages. Whatever lagging spirits were about, they had nothing to say about this curious cracked doorway.

He didn't *feel* watched. So he broke the rule. When he was patrolling the Roxbury streets and infested alleys where the specks and leavings of crime showed themselves, he always checked them out. He and his partner didn't barge through front doors. They circled round to the back. They slipped in by the side. They didn't show their faces through front windows; they moved to the side ones first.

First, check the inside from the outside—that was the rule. But he was lulled by Sarah's homey stew dinner, and Miles's harmless blather, and Jean's cozy light-in-the-night, his extravagant image of her snug in bed, reading with her long hair undressed over her half-naked shoulders and puffy pillow.

He didn't check first. When he left his listening stance and stepped across the remaining five feet to the door, his shoes broke the silence. Not much. Just enough to know that whatever sound arose came from him and was, therefore, safe. He was safe. His movement to the door overcame his wily inertia, and that too fed the sense of safety.

He reached for the knob and changed his mind. Instead, he pushed the door back with his fingers, easily. He still had the caution, all right.

Then he heard the muffled scrape of cloth against cloth behind him. The explosive rush at him. Boots hard-clawing the ground. The air compressed against his back as the charging body lunged toward him. It took seconds. Milliseconds.

The clamp of a spread-fingered hand on his head caught him with a lunging momentum and smashed his head against the door. At the same time, the other hand shoved full force between his shoulder blades. Hugh heard the muted bone-slap of his head against the yielding wooden panel and felt the exhaustion of his lungs, the blunt pain and the driving force against his back.

The door swung on its hinges like a kicked gate, and Hugh tumbled onto the floor, his knees hitting when his feet couldn't. Instinctively, he wrapped his arms around his head to avoid more pain.

The door thudded against the low dresser table behind it and bounced halfway back to the jamb. The clamor signaled more unknown torture or suffering or something horrible, but that didn't come.

A second later, Hugh rolled to the side, his knees protecting his gut. The doorway was empty. The night flowed in.

He glanced around him. He was alone.

The room was an upheaval in the dark. The bed was ransacked, mattress over the edge, spread and covers and sheets ripped off. His clothes were dumped and thrown helter-skelter. His suitcase was overturned; his shirts and socks scattered. The place was a mess, ambushed.

Boot steps sounded through the doorway, running away.

Hugh jumped up, impervious to the pain, and flung the door the rest of the way back.

He heard something off to the side, and then his eyes caught the flash of movement through the still pines. He ran after it, like an impulsive greyhound, only the rabbit he chased was the aggressor, trespasser, sneak thief in the night. Hugh ran like he used to, the 880 man, track star in college newspaper, the long-legged, lanky, bony-armed, second-place half-miler. Only it was different in the woods at night, dodging hunks of impenetrable tree trunks and eye-gouging twigs. One time he ran down a punk thief in Dorchester. Caught him red-handed snatching a boom-box radio. He simply ran him down because the punk was a monkey with his paw around a banana in a bottle; he wouldn't let go. The punk wouldn't let go of the goddamn radio.

This man was wearing dark clothes, but Hugh could see the glint of moonlight moving on him as he ran between the trees, dodging them as Hugh was doing. Except it looked easier for him, better. The terrain angled up, and Hugh felt it in his gut. The man was stretching the gap, out-distancing him. He had the lead on Hugh from the start, but he was building more besides.

Hugh knew he wasn't going to snag him. The slope steepened, and that was it—just like Heartbreak Hill in the Boston Marathon. The earth was tilting up sharper and fast. He felt it one-for-one just as fast and sharp. He kept seeing the outlined streaks slipping through the woods, silent blips of Arabic-looking glints as they wove in and out of the pines and oaks and hemlocks. And he kept running.

The slope was angling into mountain bases where boulders gradually took over. The trees dug in and gripped hard, but not as thick. He was moving into the transition edge—not quite a forest floor, not quite mountainside.

He was puffing too much, his legs giving out. The man was heading straight up the side. Hugh would never catch him.

Then those flashing glints of moonlight streaks disap-

57

peared behind a boulder, maybe into a crevice. Hugh couldn't be sure. He stopped and peered hard up ahead, straining through the darkness as if the intensity of his stare would reveal what his eyes couldn't see.

The focus tightened his mind. He stepped behind a bulky spruce tree and put his body out of sight. His breath poured out, a night animal on the hot empty prowl. He eased around the tree and saw the stillness of the mountainside. He studied the boulder where the man disappeared. It was like any number of them perched on one another and jagging the vertical lines of the trees. Maybe he was looking at the wrong one.

He listened, but it was only his breath lessening.

Let it be. It's too pat, too tempting. That killer rat in Boston disappeared in a burned-out tenement once, and Hugh kept pressing. The punk fired down the hallway and splattered the plaster behind Hugh, thigh high.

Let it be.

But he couldn't, not yet. He had no reason to think the man had a gun. If he did, he would have used it back at the cottage. He would have stopped running, turned around, and fired—fired to kill or fired to frighten. He did neither.

If he felt trapped now, maybe he would. If he had a gun. How could you tell for sure?

But who was trapped? It was Hugh who wasn't moving up the mountainside. He was the one pinned down behind the tree, easing out, showing his eyes and that's all. He was the one stopped.

The man knew the territory, not Hugh. Maybe he was taking a bead on Hugh right now and just waiting for a clear shot, a closer one, waiting until Hugh came out and climbed up the rocks, waiting for those rocks to slow Hugh down. Good targets didn't move.

No, Hugh held back. He waited and watched.

He could smell the night again, the fresh piney resin and the cold leafy tautness that came with autumn. His breath evened out. So did the racing pitch of his insides.

For a time the two running human monsters must have slowed the wildlife to a halt. They must have panicked the muskrats and porcupine, clipped off whatever sounds they made. The deer must have frozen still, heads up, ears cocked, eyes alert. But then, when the two-legged killing creatures stopped their thrashing, the wildlife got their night back. Hugh heard a creak of something down the hill behind him. He turned to it. Maybe it was a prowling beaver or a pine scraping itself in the breeze that rustled the tops of the trees but never made it down low. An owl hooted to the right. Another one answered, scaring a field mouse out hunting, frozen stiff, easy plucking.

He tried to figure the cottage scene. Simple thieving wasn't likely. The room was too trashed for that. And smashing him against the door was an extra-special coupon bargain. No simple-minded thief already outside a cottage who had already ransacked the place would take a chance on getting bagged by smashing him against the door. Not when he was already home-free—unless the guy was a psychopath.

It was a warning. In a small town, if you wanted to know where someone was, you could know right away. You could be a loner, but everyone else knew *where* you were being a loner.

A warning for what exactly? The killings, of course. Maybe Hugh had hit on something that he didn't recognize yet. Or maybe the killer thought so. Or maybe he was just an outsider nosing around too much. Outsiders were easy targets. Get them first. Get them out of town. Scare 'em off.

Maybe it was for Amy. But that was too farfetched. All he was doing was looking for her. People sometimes got twisted out of shape when somebody from outside—somebody with an official tone—came in and gritted up the place. It staggered them, got them upset. But enough to kick Hugh around? No, he doubted that.

He looked up the mountainside and saw nothing that moved.

Let it be.

He cleaned up the mess. Nothing was damaged. The mirror over the dresser was tilted; the empty drawers had been thrown to the floor. The towels in the bathroom had been heaved out of their drawers. It was clearly a nuisance attack. The floor lamp leaned at a forty-five-degree angle against the bed, its shade still intact. The throw rug beside the bed had been kicked and folded over itself.

The anger bubbled up. Being attacked, having his territory invaded, no matter how temporary, boiled him. No good. Keep your cool. Analyze it. Figure it. Find him.

Hugh had already planned to drive down the next day to see Wendall Kellor in Wellesley, Proctor's lead. The man in Dedham was too far. Besides, Wellesley had the tone for what he needed to confirm.

If he went now, the threat would seem to work. Hugh Quint cleared out at the first sign of commotion. That wasn't too keen. It encouraged assumptions for later on— Hugh Quint was an easy rabbit to scare, Hugh Quint turned tail fast. That could reap more bad bruises.

He felt the top of his head. The bash from the door was mounding up, going to be a sore one. A real sorehead. He smiled and cursed. It wouldn't show much under his hair.

On the other hand, let the man think he had scared Hugh off. Why not? Go to Wellesley. What difference did it make? Maybe it would lead to what Hugh didn't know. It was worth a try. What the hell.

Once everything was back in place, Hugh stood in the center of the room and studied it. With the bed made, everything was just the way Jean had first showed it to him. Why tell her about it? If she came by tomorrow and peeked in when he wasn't there, she wouldn't know the difference.

He looked out the side of the pulled shade. It was pitch dark. She had turned out the light.

He'd leave in the morning early. He had to find out what Kellor had to say about the Dunlap high chest. He'd leave before Jean had a chance to get up and out. Interstate practically all the way. He could skirt around deep Boston to get to Wellesley. He'd get there midmorning. Plenty of time to talk with Kellor and get back to Longfield.

Sarah's high chest of drawers was a beauty, but he needed some preliminary information before figuring it all out. Proctor was right, no doubt, but Proctor was Proctor. Kellor could tell him up close what to zero in on, what a Dunlap shouldn't have, what makes a good one worth top dollar. It might lead to something.

At first he hadn't connected the killings with the chest. Why would he? Nothing had happened with the chest, except ten or twelve years of bickering and flinty talk back and forth between the Tuckers and Coopers. But he'd changed his mind about that when the chief told him that Sarah's will was missing from Bryan's office.

8

THERE IS NO GREATER DISASTER THAN GREED.

—Lao-tzu

EARLY NEXT MORNING Hugh drove out of the White Mountains and followed the I-93 trail south through Concord, Manchester, and past neon no-taste Nashua. *Money* magazine had voted Nashua the best city in America to live in. What a joke that was. Best if you thought money meant immortality and you were Robin Hood in reverse. He turned onto Route 3 and over the Massachusetts border with the other four-wheelers heading toward heaven, so they thought. A half hour later he turned right onto Highway 128, where endless tinted-glass companies lined the high-tech loop around Boston—the illusion was that the peaceful design of death-ray weapons secured a good job; the truth was that the loop was first target on the Soviet list.

He turned right off 128, wound through the portals of suburbia, and drove into Wellesley. Driving into Wellesley was like pulling on your jodhpurs and trying to decide whether you'd like to fox hunt or play polo. The main street shone as if lined with white porcelain. No stretchy, outsized buildings here, no cloud piercers to block the sky above. Instead, the Viennese bakery, Oriental rug retailer, evening-wear clothier, and leather goods entrepreneur stationed themselves along the boulevard to do the townspeople a favor.

Wendall Kellor's shop was discreetly located one door from the main boulevard on an elegant sycamore-lined side street. In black letters outlined with gold leaf, the name of Kellor Collections suggested straightforward wealth. Abandon all hope of ticky-tacky goods and commensurate prices upon entering here.

Mr. Kellor stood imperially erect, wearing tailored dark blue suit and muted red tie, greeting Hugh with royal smile and solicitude.

"What may I do for you, Mr. Quint?" he said after introductions, a man who knew the difference between may and can.

"Perhaps I should have made an appointment," Hugh said, donning the drapery of mutual solicitation. He too could stand imperially erect. He wasn't Boston-bred for nuthin. "But I took my chances that you'd be here."

"The gods were with you."

"First, of course, I wanted to see your fine display. I've heard good words about it."

"Thank you. I trust what you see will match the words."

"I'm sure of it," Hugh said and glanced around.

The shop was carpeted in Oriental rugs. The walls were hung with obviously treasured paintings framed and lighted with museum expertise. Vases and statuettes were spaced judiciously around the showroom. One corner displayed exquisite inlaid Chinese furniture that showed highly crafted work, even from across the room. Chippendales and Hepplewhites had been positioned in handsome, shadowed light.

"Does your interest turn more to paintings or furniture?" Kellor asked with proper dealer diffidence, inserting his left hand into his coat pocket.

"Right now, furniture," Hugh said. Then he struck the golden ring. "But I'm wondering if you've added any new canvases that you particularly like?"

Kellor's eyes brightened. "As a matter of fact," he said, a fully pleased face smiling as he spoke, "I've added one of the most thrilling finds in all the years I've been in this field. Come here, I'll show you."

He led Hugh through a hallway to a second smaller showroom. Inside the doorway he stopped and pointed straight across the room to the far wall. A large dark-colored painting hung in deliberate isolation. " 'David With the Head of Goliath,' " he said.

Hugh studied it a moment. "Beautiful."

"Yes," Kellor said, "and the story behind it is as interesting as the painting is beautiful."

"Which is . . ."

He smiled. "Last year I was fortunate enough to be wandering in an antique shop in southern California when I spotted a large dusty painting in the back room. The shop was nothing like you see here, of course. Nevertheless, the style and tone of the painting, beneath all the grime, intrigued me. The more I studied it, the more I realized that this was a Valentin de Boulogne. Do you know him?"

"No."

"He was a contemporary and admirer of Caravaggio in the baroque period of the seventeenth century. Anyway, I checked a catalog to confirm, and, sure enough, it was a de Boulogne. The catalog listed it as missing."

"A real find. A discovery."

"It was," Kellor said. "I did further research and found that Cardinal Barberini commissioned the painting in sixteen twenty-seven. The painting remained in the Barberini family through the centuries until the nineteen thirties. Then it disappeared when a dealer got hold of it. From what I could find out, the painting showed up in the Yugoslavian Embassy in Madrid in nineteen thirty-eight. Then a nephew in the family bought it and gave it to a friend, a Serbian priest in Monterey Park, California. Last year when the priest moved, he gave it to the dealer with the dark showroom to sell."

"And you bought it."

"Not that easily. When I returned to the dealer he had sold the painting. Naturally, I was deflated, but not

64

dejected." He smiled at his professional determination.

"But how did you come to buy it?"

"I traced the new owner and persuaded him to part with it."

"What magical persuasion did you use?"

"Now that is a trade secret."

"You must have paid a handsome price."

"I paid double what the new owner had paid."

When Kellor paused and hung the price in front of Hugh's curiosity, Hugh played the card: "Which was . . ."

"Four thousand dollars." He smiled in triumph.

"A steal."

"You might say that."

"What is it worth now?"

"As a Caravaggesque, let us say it is worth considerably more than I paid."

"I would think so."

They let a silence end this part of the business. Then, as was the custom of gentility, Hugh glanced away, inhaled slightly, pursed his lips, and frowned—all to begin another train of thought. Two could play the game when two knew the rules.

"I was wondering," he said, "if you could provide me with a little information. I wanted to know if there is any interest in a highboy of the Dunlap school."

"Always," Kellor said evenly.

"This chest is a particularly fine example in excellent condition."

"Does it belong to you?"

"No, but I'm trying to determine its value for someone, and you were recommended to me."

"I'm pleased to hear that. It is in good condition?"

"Perfect."

"And it has some of the characteristic Dunlap features—complex cornices, the sharply creased knees, the spoon-handle shell?"

"Yes, all those, and something, I'm told, that is extraordinary. But what would a Dunlap be valued at?"

"Well," Kellor said in the customary delaying tactic, "this depends greatly on the individual piece of furniture—in this case a chest-on-chest—but if it can be authenticated as a true Dunlap, then assignment of the value must take this into consideration."

"Are we talking four thousand dollars, as in that Caravaggesque you bought?" Hugh smiled.

"I'd say slightly more."

"And if it is signed?"

Even Kellor's imperial training couldn't disguise his autonomic system. His eyes widened at the sound of the word "signed." However, he was obliged by mercantile history to say something, *anything*, to keep from scaring the prospect away by overreacting with bodily enthusiasm. The same marketing tactic that applied to ankle bracelets applied to antiques.

"Well," he said, to say something, "that always adds a modicum of extra interest, and it adds, of course, to the value."

"I understand that not many Dunlaps are signed," Hugh said, staring straight at Kellor, letting him know that rare Dunlap signatures increase the value more than a modicum, my dear man.

"Yes, that is true. This is very interesting, Mr. Quint. You may have a treasure here, but then again"—the tactic—"this all depends on the individual piece and its condition and construction and whether the signature is truly authentic."

"It is," Hugh said, and watched capitalism in a cravat show itself. Money by any other name was still money.

Kellor nodded professionally. "Where is this chest, by the way?"

"Up north," Hugh said, pokering it. "I'm just on an exploratory trip, you understand."

"Of course."

"But let's say, for purposes of discussion, that this chest is of the high period of the Dunlap school, in excellent condition, and signed. What would you suggest as its value?"

"It's very difficult to say without seeing it."

"I understand. Of course, I'm not asking you to specify exactly, and I certainly wouldn't hold you to any figure."

"I realize that. You just want a range of some sort."

Hugh nodded.

Kellor jerked his wrist in front of him, then raised his forefinger. "But first, Mr. Quint, I must make a short call. I'm terribly sorry, please forgive me. I promised to check in a few minutes ago."

"Quite all right."

Kellor moved to the doorway. "This won't take me a minute. I have to check in with my assistant. He's assessing items in an attic for a client, whom, I'm afraid, thinks his cache has much more value that it actually contains. He doesn't have a signed Dunlap chest, I'm afraid. Please make yourself comfortable."

Kellor smiled and went to his office, closing the door as he entered. True to his word, he returned shortly and found Hugh admiring the Chippendale side table against the back wall.

"A charmer, isn't it?" Kellor said.

"Yes."

"Now, where were we? Ah, yes. Of course, I don't usually give any estimate off the cuff. So much is involved. But let's say for the Dunlap that you describe, I would say its value lies somewhere between five and fifteen." The thousand, of course, was understood.

The next ten minutes were departure time. The two of them bantered and shuffled in the unWoolworth manner, each of them thankful for the other's contribution. After all, Kellor had discovered the existence of a Dunlap treasure chest. And Hugh had found out the colossal value of Sarah's Dunlap, from the naked greed revealed through this dealer's gilded facade.

Hugh drove out of Wellesley, got back onto 128, curved around Boston, and headed north to Longfield. How could he not smile at the whole Wendall Kellor scene? So familiar. It was like the lily days of yesteryear in good ol' Boston. It was where ladies didn't *buy* hats. They *had* them.

The two cars that followed him all the way up Route 3 to Nashua were part of the normal everyday fare. People commuted back and forth all the time, nothing unusual about that. In fact, they jockeyed here and there as the traffic forced them. Sometimes Hugh drove on ahead, sometimes the other cars took the lead, passing on the left, getting blocked, switching to the right lane and getting blocked again. At one point the gray Olds dropped out of sight before coming back into the rear-view mirror five minutes later. Driving long straight stretches did that.

The driver in the Toyota had to be a salesman for computers or an accountant or executive-level functionary on his way to the company branch. His jacket was flipped over the passenger seat. He wore a white dress shirt and tie.

When the three of them reached the Nashua bypass, the Toyota turned off before the toll road to Manchester. Hugh and the Olds kept going north.

A lot of people drove north. Why shouldn't an Olds?

Hugh got in the longest line in the toll booth; the Olds angled into the shortest line for the exact change. That was when he took a look up close. The driver turned to throw his coins into the toll gullet, then sped the Olds on through the raised gate. He wore an open-collar dark green shirt and had black hair, a little shaggy like the country he was driving into. In silhouette, as the man stared straight ahead again, his bushy eyebrows sprouted outward from even that distance and outlined two dark streaks above his eyes.

Hugh paid his coins and drove on. The Olds was out of sight and Hugh was reminded of the usual occupational hazard and professional malfunction—paranoia. He didn't see the Olds until six or seven miles later. It was pulled onto the shoulder, where the man was removing a leather briefcase from the trunk. Hugh watched in the rear-view mirror as the man slammed the trunk door down, walked to the driver's seat, tossed the briefcase into the car, got in, and closed the door. By the time Hugh had driven over a long rolling hill, the Olds still hadn't returned to the highway.

He got back on I-93 on the north side of Manchester, followed it through Concord, and headed into the hour-long back stretch to the White Mountains. A lot of cars followed him long distances: that was what happened on interstates. Some people found this comforting, like a commuting family. Hugh found it too coincidental, too planned. He saw the Olds speed on by him when he turned off to Longfield. The license number began with 381. It was from Massachusetts.

The note on his cottage door read: "Two messages for you—from Miles and Asa. Come see me. Anytime. Jean."

9

DAKOTAS, I AM FOR WAR.

—RED CLOUD

"ANYTIME" MEANT NOW, as far as Hugh was concerned. He hurried inside and took a quick shower to wash off Boston, just in case. Dressed and dandy, he quick-stepped to Jean's front door and knocked only once before she opened it and ushered him in.

"Hi."

"Got your note."

She told him that Miles had called frantically (what else?) to say that he *had* to see Hugh, he had a *great* idea about the chest and Amy (oh, by the way, he said, had Hugh found her yet?), and Hugh was supposed to go see him right away, as soon as he got there, no buts, right away. Jean told him that Miles said he would be waiting all night and all day for a week if he had to, until Hugh got there. He wouldn't even *eat*, that was what a great idea he had. What eating had to do with the idea, Jean said, she didn't know, but that was what he'd said to tell Hugh.

They stood in the center of the room exchanging knowing analyses of Miles Cooper. Jean said she well knew him and his ways and that fifty percent of the time he was describing reality accurately and fifty percent of the time he wasn't. The problem was to figure out which fifty percent.

Hugh laughed and agreed and then said in answer to her invitation, yes, he would like a little bite to eat, as a matter of fact. So he watched Jean make an omelette on the French tender side, sprinkle on some fresh chopped dill, slather some sweet butter onto heated slices of a fresh *baguette*, and present it alongside an open cup of apricot jam and espresso café au lait. He liked the way she moved, the glances over her shoulder, the sense of creation over the stovetop. She had nice legs, from the waist down.

She told him the other news. Asa Nickerson had stopped by and said that he wanted to meet with Hugh too. Actually, he got in touch before Miles did, but the difference between Miles and Asa made one put Miles first, like storm before calm. Asa mentioned something about getting Hugh in touch with Amy. Jean didn't know exactly what he meant, except that in his easy way Asa wanted Hugh to know and to get in touch with him. He wasn't too clear about it.

So Hugh told Jean about his experience with Asa at his cabin in the woods, the bird calls and stealth that Eric had taught him, the description of Eric himself. Hugh was beginning to understand more about this Eric Cornplanter and what was appealing about him for Amy. More was involved than Hugh first had thought. And then he realized how easy it was to talk with Jean.

They finished eating and took the dishes to the sink. She would have none of his washing the dishes. Next time, she said. He agreed, and liked knowing about a next time. They talked some more, and Hugh said he would get in touch with both Miles and Asa to make an honest messenger of her, knowing, after all, that it was not the messages that got burned but the messengers.

She followed him to the door. He put his hand on her arm. She did the same. He leaned to thank her with a kiss good-bye. Instead, she kissed him hello.

The next morning Hugh called Proctor Hammond, his tycoon of trivia, dispenser of information and dyspepsia.

Proctor grunted acknowledgment and urged Hugh to get on with it.

"Two questions," Hugh said.

Before he could continue Proctor cut in. "Number one is?"

"Don't let me hurry you, of course."

"Number one is?"

"Have you noticed anything about your telephone manner, Proctor? I mean, have you given any thought to planing some of those edges?"

"I never plane perfection. Number one is?"

"Should I start when the beep sounds?"

"Funny."

"What do you really know about this Wendall Kellor?"

"You talked to him and so now you want me to tell you what I think of him."

"You gave me his name, you know."

"He was my second recommendation, but he told you what you wanted to know."

"He told me."

"Everybody complains about something. You think he's a snake with a necktie."

"I don't know. I'm asking you."

"You wanted to know how valuable that high chest of yours—"

"—Sarah's . . ."

" . . . is. So I gave you his name and he told you. You didn't ask me whether you can trust him with a ten-foot pole. You asked me about a dealer who could tell you something about the value of a high chest. So I told you and now you blame me for all the snake trails he leaves behind. Don't blame me if he's a rattler, Quint, don't blame me."

"I'm not blaming you. What do you mean he's a rattler?"

"Don't blame me that he never got caught, don't blame me."

"Caught for what?"

"He never got caught."

"For what?"

"There can't be a what if he's not caught. I deal in facts, Quint, facts. Numbers, measurements, what *is*. I don't speculate. That's for philosophers like you."

"It's not speculation that's important. It's causes, relationships, effects, impingements. Besides, you're giving me a subtle *argumentum ad ignorantiam*. Since Kellor's innocence can't be disproved, therefore, it's probably true that he is innocent. But at the same time, you're saying it all with a subtext of he's-guilty-as-hell."

"Big words for little doings. Let's put it this way. Slick, smooth Kellor bought one hundred and five old hand-carved duck decoys from a Vermont couple on welfare for $1,157 and then turned around and sold them in his antique shop for $61,590. It's one of those classic dealer stories that every insider knows about. Wendall Kellor is very proud of that episode. That's the kind of Wendall Kellor we're talking about."

"You still haven't told me caught for what."

"You didn't ask me whether Kellor was caught for fencing a stolen Stradivarius violin, whether he is in a position as a go-between for high-finance thieves. You didn't ask me that. I gave you what you wanted and you got it."

Hugh paused. So did Proctor, until he could no longer.

"You're in catatonic shock. This news has short-circuited you, unplugged you. And you were a big Boston cop knee-deep in the sleaze of life and death of modern America. You're up there in treeland and you've forgotten that sleaze wears white shirts, Quint. Down here it's white shirts and sleaze. Bloom and rot, bloom and rot."

"How can you fence a Stradivarius?"

Proctor sniffed into the phone. "Easy. The old guy made eleven hundred instruments—viols, cellos, mandolins, guitars. The guitars are useless, worthless. Hang them on your wall. Make them into lamps. But the violins—someone bought a Strad violin smashed up in a box for thirty thousand dollars. It took another thirty thousand to put the golden egg back together again, but since it was dated after seventeen hundred when the old guy made the best of them, the money was worth it. You have thirty thousand dollars, Quint, you rich inheritable Back Bayer, but I don't."

"Sorry."

"You fence a Stradivarius like you fence anything else."

"But they're all so researched."

"And cataloged and documented and insured and photographed. So you might as well steal the Rock of Gibraltar and try to sell it at a French flea market—except for certain smudged-up dealers. Not all dealers are Bernini's angels and apostles from St. Mark's Square, little ivory-hearted Quint."

"I'm so innocent."

"A little pigeon guano falls on angels and apostles, so the question is not how but why. The answer to why is that enough rich wimps consider the gluttonous ownership of a Stradivarius more important than whether or not it is stolen. I know one rich woman wimp who bought two tiger-skin coats when she heard that Bengal tigers were going on the endangered species list, because they'd be twice as valuable—the coats, not the tigers. It's the same with Stradivarius violins."

"So how is it done?"

"Quint, the right dealer will buy the right stolen Stradivarius. The right buyer will buy the Stradivarius from the right dealer. They will find the right way, like preparing double records and receipts, ignoring the register of the Stradivarius serial number, scratching it out, disguising the great Antonio's signature, and most of all being very, very quiet about the transaction and walking on tippy toe."

"Is Wendall Kellor the right dealer?"

74

"I accuse nobody."

"You accuse me of being a nitwit, Proctor, and I'll never forget it."

"Fact, Quint, I tell you time and again. I deal in facts."

Hugh smiled at Proctor's squeaky excitement.

"What works for Stradivariuses works for Dunlap high chests. Good-bye."

"Wait."

"I'm busy."

"Coffee break, huh?"

"If you really want to know, which you don't, I'm about to recalculate Count Rumford's original figures of fireplace chimney drafts and how they fit into the venturi principles of funnels. The venturi tube is named after G.B. Venturi, who worked on hydraulics and aerodynamics. You wouldn't know."

"Right, Proctor."

"Right, Quint."

"Ever heard of the Abenaki Indians?"

"Of course, I've heard of the Abenaki Indians. They lived in the Northeast. You're sitting or standing or lying down or whatever you're doing right where they lived, only they were converted to Christianity by the French Jesuits, who allied them with the French government against the English hordes. That's why New Hampshire is New Hampshire instead of New Provence. So our beloved English ancestors obliterated their little wigwam towns and they moved to Quebec. They're still there, hundreds, thousands. I'll look it up. Give me your number there."

Hugh gave it.

"Bloom and rot, Quint. That's what it's all about. Life is bloom and rot. We bloom, we rot. Wendall Kellor blooms and then he rots. The Abenakis bloom as a civilization and then they get infected with the white-man world and they rot. Whole huge civilizations bloom and the world is a Golden Age—the Persians, the Greeks, the Romans, the

Americans. Then comes the rot, the leprosy of greed and myth and power. It's rot that rules."

"Proctor, you're a cynic, a Spengler, and he was all wet. Civilizations don't operate on time clocks like tree farms. They adjust, they rebalance. Egypt lasted three thousand years. It's still going."

"It's still going because it's still rotting. Seventeen million Americans eat at McDonald's every day. McDonald's is rotting the world. Ten thousand Golden Arches are infecting the whole world. Tokyo, Bangkok, Buenos Aires, Paris! The virus is in *Paris*."

"What has McDonald's got to do with it?"

"You see, you're exactly what I mean. An infection doesn't attack itself."

"The truth of the matter, Proctor, is that everything doesn't bloom at the same time and rot at the same time. One supports the other and that's why the cynicism of archivists is misinformed. Life lives for the bloom, Proctor, not the rot."

"Good-bye."

"It's true. Look at you. You're in one glorious bloom right now."

"Good-bye."

"I'm very impressed."

"Remember this, Quint."

"What?"

"Life is Jesus versus the Christians."

An hour later Proctor called back and poured forth what he had learned about the Abenaki tribes since he'd hung up. It was an astonishing display of sponged-in history and catastrophe, delivered in rapid-fire peals like a guru at Disney World.

Hugh had to admit, to himself at least, that Proctor Hammond did have a high-minded usefulness and that what he delivered contained value, although his uninterruptable delivery was nerve-racking. Hugh listened as Proctor spouted off about how the Abenakis were a federation of Algonquian, Passamaquoddy, and Penobscot nations against the Iroquois League of New York— before, of course, New York was New York. The Abenakis hunted, they fished, they grew maize in the eastern coastal regions—Abenaki *meant* easterners—before the English destroyed their core in 1724.

They ran trap lines for marten and mink furs, they set rabbit snares, they used bows and arrows. They covered their wigwams and canoes with birch bark. They lived peaceful lives. The chief was the chief advisor and that was it, no compulsory authority, a wise figurehead, a moral leader. Someone else was the war chief, and even then ordinary men and women—Did Hugh hear that? Men *and* women—decided in general council matters relating to war.

On and on Proctor spoke, spewing his screechy sentences into the phone. The spew was jangling, but Hugh listened with grateful silence as this instant lesson wove an understanding of these pursued people. Then Proctor mentioned something that truly perked Hugh's interest— one of those intellectual injections that prickle the body just a little, just enough to perk the mind to attention. Proctor said that throughout their history, the Abenaki had a legend of a hero who would return to the people to help them in time of great need—a savior, pure in the ways of the Abenaki, a life-saving counterforce to lead the people to restoration, rebirth, and restitution. It was a belief that persisted to the present day.

10

THESE LANDS ARE OURS. NO ONE HAS A RIGHT TO REMOVE US
BECAUSE WE WERE THE FIRST OWNERS.

—TECUMSEH

WHEN HUGH APPROACHED the clearing near Asa's cabin, he stopped in mid-stride, waiting for his presence to ignite a flurry of ersatz crow caws, like last time. No Asa crow cawed, so Hugh walked into the clearing that parted the woods like a stage for the distant mountains. A blue jay lighted on a hemlock branch and screeched at him. Another one screeched back from across the way. Then the first jay flew thirty feet to the left and up and screeched again, igniting another exchange of saucy warnings to the intruder.

Hugh stood in front of the cabin and called, "Asa?"

The weathered old man stepped from around the edge of the cabin and smiled. "That wasn't me," he said, angling his head toward the blue jays.

"I wasn't too sure about that."

"But I knew you were there. These jays here know me. They wouldn't be calling like that."

"I'm just a city boy."

"No, you're not. I can tell. Maybe some." Asa tipped his head again to the birds. "But it's confusing when you don't know enough. I was that way."

Hugh followed the man to the plank front steps and watched Asa sit down, ignoring the chair on the porch, leaning his elbows on his thighs, looking up with prescient eyes and knowing what Hugh was going to say next.

"I got your note."

Asa nodded.

And Hugh waited. This was the slow woods. Words had their season.

Finally, Asa leaned to the side to peer around Hugh. He tossed his head in slow motion again, like he had with the blue jays. In the matter-of-fact manner that surprises nobody who knows the mountains and brooks and the rhythm of the unpredictable in nature he said, "He's over there."

Hugh turned and saw the lean, black-haired man standing in front of the giant hemlock.

Eric Cornplanter.

He wore jeans and a dark brown long-sleeve shirt the color of the fallen needles at his feet. His black hair was long enough to tie back into a small strand at the nape of his neck. He stood alert and ready to move, waiting.

Then he walked across the clearing toward Hugh and Asa, his young, sturdy stride straight and smooth, light-footed and silent. Steady eyes and mouth.

He stopped three strides before Hugh and was still, almost challenging. They knew each other: greetings were for strangers or white-man business, but the silence was not ease.

This man's silence was an intensity, not the silence of men who mimicked the lulls of the woods and mountains. Hugh saw the same still face and body that marked men of this mountain breed, but the dark eyes of the Abenaki were prepared and guarded. They showed a piercing edge toward humans not usually found in skittish back-country men. Yet Hugh could see the detachment he shared with them.

What Eric said first seemed out of sync. "Welcome to our mountains."

Hugh thought he was referring to Asa and himself, but

the more he listened, the more he realized that the old loner wasn't included.

"Asa said you might know where Amy is."

Eric made no movement toward the old man sitting on the steps, leaning on his knees, making no interference. Asa was a go-between, and his part was done. He was in the penumbra now.

Finally, the Abenaki said, "I know where she is."

"Her mother is worried about her. Is she all right?"

"She's a woman here. She's all right."

"She's been missing and Sarah is worried."

"She is not missing. I know where she is."

"Where?"

Eric paused, keeping his eyes unwavering on Hugh. "We Abenaki lived in these mountains and we will live here again," he said. His voice showed the litany cadence of native people, the narrow tones that reflected the dance and song of native Americans. He spoke with the unmistakable legacy of his white-man education—the words and structure—but the content was not of those classrooms.

"These mountains are ours. They are our mother and we belong to her and she belongs to us. She is our soul, our spirit, the spirit mother of our people. We will live here again. Just as I am doing, we all will do."

The passion of his youth raised his hands to his waist, palms cupped to receive—but the fingers tightened like claws.

"We are the Abenaki," he said, his eyes on Hugh, his voice feeding itself with fire. "We are a great people. We are betrayed by destroyers of great people. We are a great people for our mother, for these mountains. We love these mountains as our mother loves us. We belong to these mountains and these mountains belong to us. Our home is these mountains, as it has been from the beginning of time. We cannot be turned away forever. We will live, all of us, in these mountains again. I will see to it."

80

He stopped suddenly, as if he were guarding against himself. Hugh saw the fire controlled, the man's hands lower to his side. He saw the Abenaki regain the peacefulness of his words and heritage, but he also heard the grip of the man's strength. The words were noble and perhaps true, but the power behind them was that of a zealot. Hugh thought of the danger of angry eloquence over a longing and inarticulate crowd.

"I understand what you're saying," Hugh said and paused, letting the pause repair what the heat had done. He felt the impulse to counterattack and defend his own heritage, to thrust out his own noble and true words. But, hell, he was there to find Amy. "What you say is important and sometime I want to hear more of what you have to say, but right now Amy is important to *her* mother."

"Her mother is these mountains," Eric said. "You tell me that you understand. Do you understand the lies and deception and treaties broken by your people? The Northwest Ordinance of seventeen eighty-seven said, 'Indian lands and property shall never be taken from them without their consent.' The General Allotment Act of eighteen eighty-seven made farmers out of wanderers and hunters. The Reorganization Act of nineteen thirty-four was a travesty upon our brothers. The Bureau of Indian Affairs herded our people onto reservations to make chained-in prisoners of free nomads, to steal our rivers and mountains, to give our people what they already had. The white man gives us places like the Abenaki Professional Park with stockbrokers and bankers—they steal even our name. You don't understand what you say you understand. Even if you understand, that is all you will do. I am *doing* something about what I understand."

Eric stared at Hugh as if he were again catching hold of himself, holding himself back.

"Where is Amy?" Hugh asked.

Eric waited, cooling the distance between them. "We

81

have a legend," he said. "A lonesome man meets a beautiful woman with long silk hair. This beautiful woman of long hair promises to remain with him if he does what she tells him. His word is his honor and when he promises her this, she knows that he will keep his promise and she will keep hers. She tells him how to make a fire and then to drag her over the burned ground when the fire has died away. She tells him that when he does this he will see her silk hair grow from the burned ground and then he will have corn seed for his use. This is how the Abenaki were given the corn that we plant and grind and eat. This is how the Abenaki know that the woman of silk hair who gave us corn seed has not forgotten us, because whenever we see her silk hair we know that she has kept her promise as we have."

Hugh listened, his Boston Brahmin cop training seeping up through his bones. This anointed man standing before him was one to watch. Was he repeating authentic Abenaki legend, or was he twisting his hold on Amy to his own purpose? What was legend, what wasn't?

"Amy has changed her name," Eric said. "She is Moonseed. She is seed of the moon, seed of a new time."

"Who changed it, Eric?"

"Our people escaped to Canada," he said instead. "Some hid in Maine, but they all will return to these mountains. This is their true home. They have forgotten much of their ways, but the woman with silk hair who gave them fire and corn has not forgotten them. She will teach them their old roots, and I will teach them their old ways, and then they will all come back here where they were born to this world."

"It's not the same as it was," Hugh said. He was going to add that his people and other natives had learned something of value from modern times, but Eric cut him off.

"Yes, the mountains are scarred with clear-cut lumber, ski trails, gondolas, asphalt, and noise," the Abenaki said, his eyes tightening. "Fake waterfalls and neon lights and everything the mountains hate. Buildings on the tops where only the spirits should live. Beer cans and junk—your people throw these things everywhere, they don't care. My people care. My people will get rid of your people because they are trespassers and destroyers. We will get rid of your people."

"My people thought much of your people, Eric," Hugh said, the edges rounded off, easing in. Why was he telling Hugh all this? "They admired your ability to organize tribes into confederations. We based our government on your example, in fact." Hugh stopped. The Albany Plan of Union, the Articles of Confederation, the Constitution borrowed from the natives. Greek city-states were similar to bands of tribes confederated together for celebrations, like the Olympic Games, or for protection against invaders like the Persians. But he didn't say it.

"Your government stole these mountains from us."

"The White Mountains are a national forest, Eric. They're owned by everyone."

"They're owned by the federal government. Our people don't own mountains and rivers."

"But you say they belong to you."

"They belong to us as we belong to them. Your government buys and sells mountains and rivers. Our people are part of the mountains and rivers. How can we buy and sell ourselves?"

Hugh let the question hang unanswered because he realized that, to Eric, it was unanswerable.

Then, during this break in the torrent of words, the thought suddenly flashed in Hugh's head. Why hadn't he thought of it before? It had to be true. He was sure of it, and without flickering away the tense momentum between them he said it before he lost its power.

"Amy is watching us, isn't she?"

Eric's eyes flared against his will. He held his stance as rigid as before, but Hugh was close enough to see the revelation that he couldn't control. Eric's stare became doubly forced. Outmaneuvered.

"She is called Moonseed. Her name is Moonseed."

"She's watching us, isn't she, Eric?" Hugh wanted to see Eric's devastation at being discovered, but all he saw was Eric's resistance against a new assessment of what this white man could do. "Moonseed is here someplace, isn't she?" Hugh said, conciliating, turning his eyes toward the woods as a gesture more than a search.

"She's here."

"Tell her to come out. I want to talk with her, just talk."

"She doesn't want to talk with you."

"How can you tell?"

"I know what she wants."

"Then show her to me. Let me see her. Let me see that she's all right."

"She's all right. She's with me. She's part of these mountains. I'm teaching her. She's part of my people. She's Abenaki. She belongs here."

"She's half Abenaki."

"The half that makes her whole."

"I just want to see her," Hugh said, and looked again toward the woods.

"You'll see her when she wants to see you. She belongs to my people. She belongs to the Abenaki."

"You mean she belongs to you."

Eric said nothing. He paused, unswayed. Then he stepped back twice, turned around, and walked away, his flat steps astoundingly inaudible and cautious.

Hugh saw his only direct link to Amy move out of reach. He had nothing to hold Eric with, no persuasion, no evidence, his chance draining away.

Hugh called out to stop him: "Eric. What are you teaching her? How to kill?"

Eric turned around, in the same fluid way he walked, and stopped. He said nothing and gave no notice of what was

84

right or wrong. He was too far away for the white man to see his eyes. He was his own answer, and it was still undecipherable. He walked toward the giant hemlock.

Hugh's chance was fading away fast. He looked at the woods in search of some unnatural color that was Amy— an exposed shirt or unnatural angle that meant a human being spying from a tree or boulder, witness in secret. She could be anywhere. Behind him. Where Eric was walking.

Hugh saw nothing. She was there, he was convinced of it, but he was no more indoctrinated in the mountains than Eric was in the Ritz Carlton. He felt fettered by his own inadequacy. Living with nature was simple, except up close. He did what instinct made him do. "AMY!"

The woods broke with the shout, shattering their seclusion.

Eric never turned around, but the speed of his reaction and wits caught Hugh by surprise. The screechy warning call of a blue jay sounded from Eric's mouth, and immediately a flurry of counter calls erupted in the woods. A blue jay in one of the high spruces bent its neck and squawked at Eric, and Hugh saw the bird. But other jay calls sounded high up in the slanting mountain woods. Among these, Hugh knew, was Amy's undetected answer and signal of escape.

Eric looked over his shoulder while the birds continued what he had started. Then he walked into the thickening woods. Hugh watched Eric Cornplanter weave in and out of the tree trunks until the colors of his clothes meshed with the trees and shadows, until finally his movements disappeared altogether.

He turned around to Asa, still sitting as before, still listening, intent in benign old wisdom. Now Hugh knew about the blue jay calls, and he remembered what Asa had said when Hugh first stepped into the clearing—that Asa wasn't the one making that blue jay call, the one not seen.

When the jays calmed down, Hugh gave up looking at

85

the woods and dismissed the idea of following Eric. That would have been like a turtle after an antelope.

He looked at Asa and pursed his lips, half grin, half chagrin.

Asa looked back at him with sympathetic grandfather eyes that said Hugh had done all he could.

11

THE ESSENCE OF LYING IS IN DECEPTION, NOT IN WORDS.
—JOHN RUSKIN

ON THE WAY to see Miles, Hugh drove past a huge boulder that outcropped the road and shifted his mind away from figuring how to track down Eric. The Greeks had their own Promethean legend of fire-giver and savior of their people, and even before that glorious civilization, trickery abounded among the cunning deities. Cronus, a god of time and fertility, swallowed his own children because an oracle told him that his sons and daughters would rise up and overthrow him. His wife, Rhea, devastated by the horrible prospect of losing yet another child in this unspeakable manner, this time gave birth to Zeus in a secluded forest where he could be hidden and protected. When the time came for Rhea to show Cronus his new son, whom he would surely devour, she offered him a large stone wrapped in swaddling clothes instead. Cronus immediately grabbed the offering and swallowed it, never realizing the difference, thus sealing his fate.

The deception Eric perpetrated on Hugh was also expert, a sign of calculating obsession. Who could tell what power he had over Amy, or how persuasive his appeal to her heritage might be? He was pitting the mother of his people against Sarah, bloodline against loving mother. A dilemma like this could tear Amy apart, split her sense of loyalty into shreds. Then Eric himself could repatch her the way he wanted. Meanwhile, he was setting himself up as the hero from a nether land who appeared in times of crisis to lead his people back to glory—his own Adam, set on making Amy his Eve, the primeval couple to rein- vigorate the race.

And then came Miles, the smiling trickster Hermes, an Olympian god-child about whom a poet such as Julia Older would write. At the age of two, Hermes stole Zeus's cattle. Zeus was angry, of course, but he thought the theft was a cute and astute enterprise for little Hermes to undertake. When Hermes grew up, Hades, the god of the underworld, taught the trickster how to wear the mask of invisibility so that he could steal anything at any time—like Miles. Along with the skill of trickery came the flighty quality of mercury or quicksilver, the charming shiftiness of the slick and the quick—like Miles.

On the other hand, Miles was the man whose trickery was by consent of the tricked, and the more outlandish the better. His schemes had begun early. Hugh remembered the time in college that Miles put forth his elaborate design to get rid of the Communists and free the whole planet once and for all. First, he said, you have to position all the free world capitalists on the right side of the planet—the western side, of course, preferably centered on Los An- geles. Everyone shouted and laughed and guffawed and said Miles was going crazy again, typical Miles, typical dodo bird Miles the magician. But Miles kept right on going, swinging his arms in earnest, battling the ridicule of his pointing classmates as he engineered his final answer to the sins against the free world.

"Here's what you do," he'd said. "You take everybody in the free world and herd them together for just a day for humanity, one measly day in the service of the human race. They can go back to being self-slobs tomorrow. One day, that's all, so all the capitalists are clustered together, on the right half of the planet earth. On the count of three, which is blasted everywhere on this half of the planet by loudspeakers, maybe

88

even from the satellites—which is easy, we can do it—on the count of three everybody jumps up. Then when everybody lands again, the impact of all those capitalists hitting the earth at the same time sends a tremendous gigantic shock wave straight through the iron core of the planet to the other side and knocks off all the Communists straight into eternal space forever—gone, disappeared, good-bye. And Los Angeles is stomped into dust besides."

Of course, everybody had laughed and jeered and thrown pencils and paper clips at Miles, but he'd said it would work, except nobody had brains enough to try it. Yeah, somebody had said, what if the impact isn't enough to overcome the law of gravity and the Communists start falling back. When they hit the earth, the capitalists will be bounced off the planet. What about that? It could go on forever, back and forth, people bouncing back and forth off the earth until the end of time.

But that's the beauty of it, shouted Miles, man against the ignorant hordes. That's when population increase is vital to the survival of the human race, which means the capitalists. The more capitalists, the bigger the impact to bounce the Communists off the world. That's the reason we have to double and triple the capitalist population or we're doomed. That's when we get all the capitalist women together and we tell them—for the good of humanity, submit or else.

Miles intercepted Hugh talking to Sarah on the porch and dragged him off to the barn laboratory while Sarah in her long blue bib apron called out, "Miles, you leave that man alone, you hear me?"

"I have to see him first," Miles called back, tugging Hugh by the sleeve, pulling him away from the porch. "It's absolutely vital. Vital!"

"Miles, you let go of Hugh right this minute, you hear me? You let him go!"

"Mother!"

"Hugh!" she called.

Hugh twisted, looking over his shoulder at Sarah and feeling like a total third grader.

"Miles!"

"Mother, I have to see him first." He tugged Hugh faster, hurrying the two of them out of earshot.

"You bring him back here, Miles, or you're going to get the living daylights whipped out of you! You won't get another piece of bread out of me, you hear that, Miles? I'll never bake you another piece of pie ever again, as long as I live, you scalawag, you."

"Judas, Miles."

"Come on, come on, I got a great idea about that high chest. You got my message, right?"

"Right."

Miles swung open the barn door, motioned Hugh with a windmill of his arm to hurry inside, and slammed the door, but not without peeking out at his mother scowling from the side of the porch.

"She just wants to feed you something," he said. Then he kicked an empty joint compound bucket out of the way and it went banging and tumbling against a dented rusted sheet metal stove that echoed back.

"All right, what is it?"

Miles faced Hugh and smiled out his confidence at the plan he was about to expose. But first he positioned his arm flat on top of a work table and swept it across like a windshield wiper: screwdrivers, nails, jar caps, wallpaper scrapers cascaded and clanked onto the floor.

Hugh waited for him to spread something on the table. He didn't. Drama and junk were just part of his trade. Put them together and out came Miles Cooper.

"I know how to get at least half the money for that chest," he said, his eyes hungry for the touch of that wealth. He waited for Hugh's reaction, as if saying the

90

words were enough to make them true.

Hugh sighed and glanced at the colossal mishmash of the barn. "Miles, you have some good ideas. That isn't one of them."

"How do you know? You haven't heard it."

"I don't have to hear it. Whatever it is, it's impossible. The chest is signed over to Amy—all of it."

"That's just it," he said triumphantly. "She's my *half*-sister! Mother can't give it all to her. She can only give *half* of it to her. Figure it out."

"That's totally ridiculous."

"It makes sense. She's my *half*-sister. She gets only *half* the chest. I get the other half. She has to sign over half to me, and I can do whatever I want with my half."

"What are you going to do? Saw it in half? What about your mother?"

"She won't come out here. She never does."

"I don't mean that. Your mother has the say in what she does with that chest. It's hers."

"You can't give all of something to half of something," Miles said. He raised his arms. "So that's it. Do you see what I mean? Do you get it?"

Hugh stepped to the door. "I get it, but you won't, Miles. Work on something else. Sarah wants to see me."

Miles followed Hugh to the door. "The thing is, Amy doesn't need that chest and I do. So I get a lawyer who says she's my half sister, she gets half the chest, I get the other half."

"It's Amy's—all of it—because Sarah signed it over to her. *All* of it, Miles."

"Amy can sell it," he said without listening, "and keep half the money. She can use it for running off with that Eric Indian."

Hugh stopped short. "How do you know she's done that?"

"She's always running off with somebody. She's a half sister, Hugh, she's half Abenaki. What do you think she does?"

"How do you know about Eric?"

"I know things, like half sister, half chest. Come on, Hugh. That's what I need—a good Boston lawyer. Give me a good Boston lawyer."

"You'd waste your money."

"He'll do it on a contingency basis."

"Hell, no, Miles, any lawyer would laugh you out of town."

"I'll give you ten percent."

"Forget it."

"Fifteen percent. How about fifteen percent?"

Hugh shook his head and grinned.

"Huh?" Miles said, grinning back. "Fifteen percent?"

"Fifteen percent of nothing, Miles, is a pain in the ass." Hugh opened the door.

"It's a pain in the ass because fifteen percent of a fortune—I'm telling you, a fortune—puts a big fat bump in your wallet and *that's* the pain in the ass. You'll be sitting on so much money once I get this electric auto battery into prototype that you'll have *two* pains in the ass."

"I got one right now, and that's enough," Hugh said. "Sarah can write her will the way she wants to. The high chest is hers."

"How do you know? Where's the bill of goods? Where's the evidence? Where's the transaction?"

"It was a poker game. It's long settled."

"Where's the will then?"

High sighed tolerance. "Miles."

"Twenty percent. How can I go over twenty percent?"

Hugh walked outside. Miles Cooper followed along like a cocker spaniel negotiating over a filet mignon.

When Sarah, who obviously was watching out the window for the two of them to reappear, came onto the porch, she stood wringing her hands in her apron and scowling at her son. As the two men approached, her scowl turned to a sweet smile directed at Hugh. She ignored Miles with aplomb.

"Hugh dear," she said, taking his arm and weaving it into hers, "I'm so glad you're here. I'm worried about Amy."

"I know you are, and I'm making some progress on it. I've just talked with some people." He decided not to mention Eric.

"I know you care about Amy. But I want to tell you what happened." She led him through the front door, and showed Miles the flat of her back.

"What's that, Sarah?"

"Now first," she said, eyes bright and admiring, head bent upward in an extravagant show of warmth so that her scalawag of a son Miles could see it all, "you have to eat something."

Miles called loud enough to sweep the words past Sarah's deliberate back. "What'd I tell you? Did I tell you that or what?"

"I don't hear you, Miles," she said. Her tone changed: "Now, Hugh, you just sit down there. You can't eat standing up or the food'll go right to your feet and you'll get fat legs."

"I wouldn't doubt it," Hugh said. "What happened? What do you mean?"

Miles sat across from Hugh at the dining-room table, with Sarah at the kitchen door. "Why do you always have to feed him? He's not a little boy, you know."

"That's right, Miles Cooper," she said, unable to ignore him anymore. "You're the boy, a big bad boy." She turned on her heel and went into the kitchen.

Miles's shoulders collapsed and he hung his suffering beagle-faced head for Hugh to see the living torment he had to face every fleeting minute of his life.

"Hugh, I know *you'll* listen to me," she called and opened the refrigerator. She returned to the doorway. "Won't you?"

Hugh suppressed his grin at the sight of her. "Always."

"Well, I'll tell you what happened, and I don't like it."

93

Miles tapped his chest. "Watch. It's about me," he said to Hugh. "Just watch."

"It's not about you, Miles Cooper," she said, "because it's about *something*."

"Did you hear that?" he said, eyebrows flipped up, mocked into anguish. "Did you hear that?"

"He thinks everything is about him," she said to Hugh.

"It's about me because it's *not* about me," he said to Hugh.

Hugh grinned and shook his head. "Go ahead, Sarah."

"Well, as I said, I was here and this man knocked on the door. Of course, I could see him drive up and get out of that car of his. He tried to play dumb, but I could tell he knew where he was. I watched him come up the steps and I let him knock. Then I answered the door, only I had something boiling on the stove, some late garden vegetables I was putting up. He tried to look like he was in town someplace and just going down street, but I knew better."

Miles tilted his tired, listening body, propped his somnolent head on his hand.

"Don't you bother me about it, Miles," she said, directing a look of motherly venom at her vexatious son. "I'll get to it."

"You didn't recognize him?" Hugh asked, mostly to counteract the extravagance of her son's antics.

"No. Then he said—all smiles, but not the kind I like, I tell you that—he said things about this and that, and then he said he'd heard about my Dunlap high chest. He was the eastern representative for an auction house in California—Beverly Hills or someplace rich, I can't remember, because I knew he wasn't any such thing. He asked if it was true I had a Dunlap high chest—a highboy."

"And you told him yes, didn't you?" Miles said, swinging around. "Why didn't you tell me about this?"

"Of course I said yes. I don't lie, Miles Cooper, like some people I know."

94

"Then what, Sarah?"

"Then he asked to see it," she said, eyes back to Hugh. "He said he'd like to admire it. I know about these people. But I wasn't going to let just anybody inside. So I asked to see his card. He showed me a card that was all embossed and in gold ink and looked all fancy and everything."

"It was a fake," Miles said.

"How do you know? Were you there?"

"Then what, Sarah?"

She smiled at Hugh, a smile that said he knew that she was proud to have such an old high chest that people were interested in. "Then I thought this would be a good easy way to have it appraised. I could tell Amy"—she glanced at Miles—"how much it was worth. Then I let him admire it, the way he said."

"Mother, why did you do that? How do you know who he is? You let him in the house! You let him *see* it!"

"I let you in."

Miles exhaled.

"Who was it, Sarah? Did you get his name?"

"No, of course not."

Miles bolted upright again. "You didn't get his name? You didn't get his *name*? What about his card? Did you keep that card?"

"No, I didn't get his name. And you said his card was a fake. Why should I? I knew I wasn't going to sell it. That's what he wanted, I know that. What do I want his name for?"

"How do you know who he was then?" Miles pleaded. "Now you don't *know*."

"Good."

"Good?" Miles said, and then turned helplessly to Hugh. "Did you hear that? 'Good!' "

"I know what he looked like, that's all I need to know."

"And he didn't give you an appraisal, did he?"

"He did too. He said he'd send it to me."

Miles bobbed his head in exaggerated exasperation.

"What'd he look like, Sarah?" Hugh asked, the question more a courtesy than anything else—until she described the man: a sort of medium kind of man, city-looking even though he wore an outdoor dark green shirt, black hair, sort of maybe not nice, sort of kind of not too friendly even though he smiled at her.

"And bushy eyebrows."

12

NOR JEALOUSY WAS UNDERSTOOD,
THE INJURED LOVER'S HELL.

—JOHN MILTON

THE MAN WITH the bushy eyebrows hadn't been merely traveling the same direction as Hugh from Wellesley to Longfield, he had been following. It fit. Wendall Kellor made that quick phone call when Hugh was talking with him about the high chest. The call was to this bushy-eyed tracker—maybe. Probably.

Hugh assured Sarah that the man undoubtedly was someone just trying to hunt down antiques in the old country houses in the White Mountains, and if she didn't want to sell she didn't have to sell. But inside Hugh felt grit rubbing the wrong way. Kellor was a slick opportunist all right, quick on the uptake, quick at treasure hunting. Proctor was right. But how did this punk connect with the killings? He'd come on the scene too late.

Then Hugh assured Miles that he had Amy to find and that he wasn't the one to talk about what to do with the high chest. That got Miles into trouble again. Hugh saw Sarah giving it to him on the porch just before Miles ran off toward his laboratory barn, and Hugh drove off to the Tuckers'.

By the time he reached the Tucker place back in the deep shadows of the woods, he knew Calvin was the one he had to persuade. Maybe it wouldn't take much, if Jean was right. The boy had fire in his eyes.

Hugh got out of his Audi. Nobody there. The mangy old mongrel got to its tired feet, then decided it wasn't worth pawing across the oil-soaked drive; he didn't even bark.

A hammer clanked against iron around the far side of the barn, and out stepped Toop Tucker, looking a lot like the mangy dog. He wore the same smudged coverall and blackened boots as last time, his beard shaved off maybe two days ago, hair hanging here and there. He stared at Hugh.

Hugh stepped toward him, and then he saw Zeta walk her proud stride from behind the house where clothes were hanging and drying in the wind. "Well, if it ain't Mr. Detective," she said, brushing her hands together, getting something off. "What brings you way out here?"

"Hello, Zeta."

She stepped up to him and faced right off, in her no-monkeyshines yellow print dress and heavy shoes. "They catch who done it yet?" she asked, those needle eyes of hers never letting go of anybody, never, no sir.

He shook his head. "Not yet."

"You mean *never*," she said, shaking her head and pursing her lips so that her hairpin mouth turned upside down. "They ain't going to catch whoever. Anybody can figure that out. Out here nobody catches nobody. Especially if he's Indian."

Toop approached, wiping his caked hands on a red oil rag.

"Toop," Hugh said and nodded. "Actually, I was looking for Calvin. Is he around?"

"He's working," Toop said, and stuffed the oil rag into his back pocket. "Cutting." He angled his head to the side.

"Don't want to see *us*, huh?" Zeta said, tossing her head back and cackling high and loud, showing her scattered empty teeth sockets. "Maybe he's finding some more hanging bodies."

"That ain't funny," Toop said. Then he quickly added, as

if the possibility were real, "He's just working. You want to go out there?"

"He don't want to go out there," Zeta said in slow motion. "Besides, he'd get lost and then we'd have to go find him." She turned to Hugh. "Wouldn't we?"

"He can find his way," Toop countered.

"What do you want to see him about?" Zeta asked.

"That's his business, woman. Lay off him. He's here to see Calvin."

Hugh kept turning his head from one to the other.

"I know he's here to see Calvin. I got ears."

"You want to see him, go out there?"

"He don't want to go out there," Zeta said, needle eyes getting into the tight stitching cycle.

"Will you let him speak?" Toop said, shifting weight to his right leg. "God, woman."

"I am!" Zeta said and clamped her mouth like a clam.

"Well," Hugh said, "maybe I can go see him. Where is he?"

"Far out," Zeta said.

"He ain't that far out," Toop said.

"Far out for Mr. Detective here," Zeta said. "I know how far out he is, and he's far out there. Let him work." She presented her dynamo stance to Hugh again. "What do you want to see him about? We'll tell him."

"God, woman."

Hugh looked straight back at her. "I'll call him tonight. When will he be back here?"

"We don't answer the phone all the time. We don't have to answer no telephone just because it rings, you know. City people have to answer telephones."

She conveyed that message just fine, all right, and Hugh got it. He smiled a little and debated the issue, then came down on the affirmative. "It's about Amy."

"You want Calvin to help you, that's what it is," Zeta said, quick as a fox. "You're still looking for her. That's it.

You can't find her 'cause she's with that Eric critter some-where and you want Calvin to find her. Ol' Mrs. Proper is all worried about her Amy flying off with that Indian man, turning into an aborigine."

"Abenaki," Toop corrected.

"I know that," she snapped back, "and so does Mrs. Proper, getting all steamed up about her, only I know bet-ter. She's more worried about that high chest of *mine* than that Amy of hers."

"Don't start on that again, woman," Toop said and walked away. "I don't want to hear it."

"I ain't the one who gave it away," she said, jutting her hen-nose after him, "Mr. Gambling Man."

Toop shoved his big black hand backward.

She directed her attention back to Hugh and kept it loud. "Mr. Gambling Man there knows what I'm talking about."

Then, as if Toop Tucker had decided to burst back on the scene with his own hulking presence and ignite himself into towering action, he wheeled around and focused on Hugh.

"Calvin'll help," he said, stepping half in front of Zeta. "He knows these woods around here like that Indian. Bet-ter. And he'll track down Amy and bring her back for *Sarah*." He glanced at Zeta. "And if he doesn't, I will, be-cause I know these mountains just as much. Besides, we don't like people like that Eric sneaking around out here, and we don't like people getting killed around here, and who knows who's doing it too. So I'll get him to help you. You can bet on that."

Zeta sniffed loud and clear. No skin off her back.

"You can *bet* on that," Toop emphasized, aiming his bull's-eye straight at her.

Yeah, well, no skin off her back.

* * *

Jean welcomed Hugh with a bright smile and a very open door. Her hands were smeared with dabs of blues and

100

purples, and when she took up an old dish towel abandoned to the purpose to wipe her fingers clean, he liked the way she did it a lot better than the way Toop did it.

"You're painting a masterpiece," Hugh said.

"I'm painting," she said, holding up her hands, "but I'm afraid the masterpiece is still in the tubes."

They smiled the message that it was good to see each other, and off she went to fix some orange-flavored tea while he lingered around her, smelled the auburn scent of her hair, or so he thought, took in quick savorings of her long neck as she reached high for the cups, leaned back against the sink so she had to come willingly—by all visible and audible accounts—close by since the kitchen was bigger for this than it ought to be.

Yes, he did like the way she moved. Yes, indeed. The importance of finding out about Calvin from Jean lost its immediacy the more he was with her. Those eyes and sweet lips. What are they like closed and open?

Why do men undervalue slow women?

Because it's for their own good.

Naw.

She asked about Amy and what Hugh had found out, about Asa Nickerson and Eric Cornplanter, about what was going on with these awful killings and if the police had any clues or were doing anything, about Sarah and Miles, about Toop and Zeta, and what about Calvin?

"That's one thing I wanted to find out from you, about Calvin. Do you think he could track down Amy? There's bad blood between Eric and him, isn't there?"

"Yes," she said in that warm liquid way of hers, "There is, and that's what worries me about those two. Amy is caught in the middle, but not only between Eric and Calvin, between Eric and Sarah too. It's not good, Hugh."

He liked his name coming from her. She thought he was smiling at the accuracy of her assessment, but it was really the way she had said his name.

101

"Let's put it this way," he said. "If Calvin finds Amy with Eric, tracks them down someplace, can he handle it? Can he keep it in? Do you know what I mean?"

She nodded; she knew. Then she shook her head. She didn't know. "You have to remember that Amy went off with Eric, not Calvin. It probably seems to Calvin that Eric stole her away from him. You know what that can do to someone like Calvin."

Hugh nodded, a confession of a tormented boyhood of his own.

She reached over to touch his hand. "You also have to remember another thing," she said. "Calvin belongs in the mountains, in the woods. He's worked there all his life, and he's worked there alone mostly. That's why he's there. He *can* be alone. He wants to be. He doesn't have to deal with people."

"There's a reason people like him are in the woods."

She nodded, withdrawing her hand as if it had done its job. "Exactly."

He did like those long eyelashes of hers.

"These people are different," she continued. "Calvin is one of them."

"What I want to find out is if he does find Eric and Amy, how's he going to react? I don't want to end up with a couple of dead Romeos and one Juliet on my hands."

"Who can say? It depends on how long he's been simmering inside."

"He was pretty matter-of-fact with that killing he found."

"I know."

They let that sink in.

"Besides," she said, "maybe seeing Amy with Eric won't be as traumatic as you think."

Hugh waited.

"Maybe he already knows where they are."

Good point: don't underestimate Calvin Tucker. She

was right. He may have tracked Amy down already, especially when he found out that Hugh was searching for her.

"Show me your painting," Hugh said suddenly, the switch of interest coming out of nowhere.

She smiled. She liked that. She got up as fast as he had said it. "Over here," she said, "but it's against my principles."

"Which one?"

"Showing strangers my works in progress."

"How can we change that?" he asked and grabbed her hand, stopping her as she passed. He wanted to think her warm hand was for him, but it was from the teacup. "This stranger business."

"I don't know. How can we?"

"It's a real problem." he pulled her hand, and the rest of her, toward him.

"It is?"

No stop signs in the way. He wrapped her hand and her arm around his waist. "Well, not always." Her other arm did the same on its own.

"Oh? Why not?"

He wrapped his arms around her waist in return. He smiled.

"You're not concentrating," she said.

"Not on the problem."

"Why not?"

"I forget what the problem is."

She smiled and kept quiet while he bent down and kissed her lightly for introduction. Then he kissed her hard for good, and the heat opened them up. Her arm slid up his back and around his neck, holding him tight and close, holding herself onto him. He tightened his hold on her, until his hand slid down the side of her waist to the crest of her hip, curvy and comfortable.

Curves began it all. And heat. But too hot too soon wasn't one of Jean's abiding principles.

"Tomorrow is another day," she said, pulling away.

He smiled. "But I haven't seen your painting. I have to see your painting-in-progress."

She laughed and said at the door, "Good night."

13

LIKE A DOG, HE HUNTS IN DREAMS.
                    —ALFRED LORD TENNYSON

HUGH DIALED THE Tucker number, but not before looking out the window and seeing—in his lonely mind's eye—Jean behind the lighted curtained bedroom window as she curled up in her sumptuous covers, her hair unloosed on the downy pillow, her silky pale blue nightgown as transparent as it was liftable.

Calvin answered.

Yes, Calvin expected him to call. Yes, he would take Hugh out to find Amy. Be at his place at five in the morning.

Calvin was sitting under an ancient farmstead maple tree across from the barn when Hugh drove up. A rifle was propped against the tree trunk.

Toop opened the house door and Zeta came out on the granite slab step, pushing the door open wider and getting past Toop. They stared at Calvin and Hugh headed down the road, the same one alongside which Danny Mayes had been hanging by a rope.

Calvin walked with long strides, the rifle swinging by his side. Hugh said nothing about it at first, but the .30-06 Winchester was a hard-hitting caliber and the .38 tucked inside the back of his own belt wasn't any match.

Calvin only answered questions, and the answers were quick and clipped. He didn't offer anything about the rifle. He let Hugh take for granted that this was Calvin's territory. This was the wild side of the mountain. This was where nature let loose and sometimes a man had to protect himself.

Finally, Hugh eased it out. "Any bear around here?"

"Some," Calvin said. "Black bear sometimes." He didn't lift the rifle a little to explain the weapon in terms of bear. He didn't gesture toward it or mention it.

They walked on the tote road following the rolling lay of the land at the base of the mountain. Early morning thickened the air with moisture. Driving out, Hugh had seen fog enshrouding the peaks, slicing off the layers of the range like a giant butcher knife, leaving the base a muted blood red from the fall colors and the rest blotched out in gray. Fog deadened sounds too, more than the usual early morning air did in the first place.

At a Y-junction Calvin pointed the rifle to the left, and they walked on as the road angled north. A quarter-mile later the terrain tilted up and walking became an effort.

Hugh let Calvin figure that he knew nothing of what Calvin felt about Amy. Maybe Hugh knew, maybe not. He didn't like that rifle, though.

"How much do you know about Eric?" Hugh asked. The road was narrowing, almost disappearing. He had to wait for the answer.

"A little," Calvin said, keeping his eyes forward, his pace exact.

"Sarah is worried about Amy," Hugh said, to mention her name, indirectly.

Calvin nodded and kept on walking without turning his head.

When the road ended abruptly, Calvin crossed in front of Hugh and led him up a footpath that angled off the edge of the road. This was a tighter incline now. Hugh was breathing through his mouth.

The maples and oaks thinned out where a long stretch of spruce and pines had grown in fast from a clear-cutting a hundred years ago or maybe only fifty.

106

The path turned to needles, some of it rain-washed clear to the sand beneath.

Up ahead Calvin looked down and pointed the rifle at a pair of gouges in the thin soil. "Deer."

The air was gauzy; they were sieving through it. It encased the woods, and only their muffled footsteps sounded, mostly Hugh's.

As they walked between two hefty white pine trunks, Hugh asked, "Do you have an idea where they are?"

This time Calvin turned his head to his shoulder and said, "Yeah."

The trail faded away. What was left was pure terrain. Calvin followed a winding route through and around outcrops of moss-encrusted boulders, up steep inclines, and through scatterings of thin grasses struggling in the meager sunlight of air shafts where an old timber had rotted and fallen before seeding itself there.

They climbed up angled slabs of ice-split granite, using two hands the steeper they climbed, their lug soles gripping the jagged stone. Not once did they walk past a ridge clearing, not once did they reveal themselves to the distance and other people's eyes.

This was a gorge of the White Mountains that Hugh had never seen or known. The morning air had the same pine-maple sweetness, but the isolation and ruggedness were beyond what he had anticipated. This was a wild place, an intimidating series of cul-de-sacs.

A huge scarlet-topped mushroom was half eaten— maybe by the same red squirrel that leaped across the branches to the left. Calvin paid no attention, but up ahead he pointed the rifle again to the ground, this time at scat.

"Fisher," he said.

Once over the second ridge Calvin said what Hugh wanted to hear. "Over there," he said, pointing the rifle through the ragged line of sight toward another ridge.

The sun still lingered back against the steep mountainsides. On some days it wouldn't be strong enough to clear away the summit fog. When they reached the other ridge, Calvin stopped. This time he looked at Hugh with tight eyes and straight mouth. "You have to be quiet. Maybe over there," he said, motioning toward the alternating lines of treetops.

Maybe he was guessing, maybe not. Hugh nodded, and the two of them hiked on. Hugh noticed that Calvin's back was slightly hunched, as if the proximity to Eric and Amy had made his body crouch for quick reflexes. It made Hugh feel too tall, too exposed. He was making too much noise walking through this silence, too much disturbance.

At the top of the second ridge where the tree line above them slanted down and the terrain at their feet shrank away, Calvin put his hand back and patted the air for Hugh to be quiet, to stop as he did. The gesture was alarmingly gentle, an incredible twist of revelation of this hunter.

Hugh did as Calvin had done—froze motionless like the cul-de-sac universe they were in, trick of the hunted deer, listening, watching, quickening the heart. The stance was absurd when it produced no results.

Utterly still, Hugh was suddenly flooded with a realization of his own vulnerability. Calvin wagged his fingers to move forward, quietly, very cautiously.

At the cluster of boulders, one of them spiked off-center by a deformed pine trunk, Calvin crouched low, careful not to touch the boulder with his rifle. He lifted the palm of his hand for total silence, studied Hugh's eyes, assessing the mettle in them, and then dotted his index finger slightly up and over the boulder.

Hugh remembered the night he and his partner had tracked down a kid thug in a burned-out Roxbury tenement. The punk had smashed open a side window of an appliance repair shop—TVs and stereos—and tried to run off with a VCR. On opposite sides, Hugh and his partner were walking the street and shaking hands with doorknobs. It was boring—that was

108

what police work was turning out to be. He heard the shattering glass half a block away. The stillness that followed was deceptive. The thug could have been feet away.

Hugh ran down the empty street, his heels thudding along the cement with more noise than he imagined they could give. He ran across the street. No cars. A passed-out drunk in the corner doorway. That unmistakable quick flash of broken glass followed by the tinkle of shards on the cement or asphalt or brick. He ran to the alley and stopped short. No more noise.

When he edged fast around the corner, he saw the punk reaching into the window, his arms straight and separated, hands gripped onto something he was lifting out.

Hugh stepped into the alley, crouched, his pistol in his right hand, steadied by his left.

"Police!" he'd shouted.

The kid let loose his grip fast, ducked, squirmed behind the iron dumpster, and slipped around the corner. Gone. A pro. Experienced, quick.

Hugh's partner, down a block on the other side of the street, ran to the alley, but was too late to go around, too late to know what was happening.

Automatically, Hugh half ran down the black tunnel alley while his partner steadied his pistol. Hugh looked back: his partner motioned that he was heading around the corner to head off the thief, killer, who knew for sure?

No, Hugh said with a slice of his hand. He knew the alley; dead-end wall. He motioned for his partner to come on up.

The two of them crouched on either side of the dumpster. No noise. Nothing.

Hugh lifted his finger toward the top of the dumpster and motioned that the punk was there, around the corner, dead-end trapped.

He wasn't. A stack of pallets was piled halfway up the wall. Perfect for climbing up and over. They weren't supposed to be there. The punk was long gone.

Calvin motioned again for silence. It was plain that he didn't think Hugh had it in him. Then he eased up, stretching his body back to full length, keeping the inches clear between himself and the boulder until he could see. He studied the other side.

Hugh lifted up, copying the stealth, knowing the city training he had that Calvin didn't know about, realizing that some of it could be used in the mountains.

They stared at the shadowed distance. When Hugh saw nothing striking, he turned questioningly, silently, to Calvin, who motioned straight ahead.

Hugh saw a bank of granite in a semicircle with pines growing on either side and dead limbs and brush fallen over each other. He looked again at Calvin. What?

Calvin studied the scene, his eyes blue-alert and sweeping from one end of the semicircle to the other. Nothing twitched on his face, no squinting, no clenching of his mouth, just the noiseless beat of his eyelids.

"There," he whispered.

Hugh looked where Calvin was staring. That helter-skelter pile of dead tree limbs and brush against the boulders was the shelter. Hugh turned and asked with his eyes if Calvin was sure.

Calvin nodded.

As far as Hugh was concerned, nothing human was set up there. It didn't make sense.

"Over there," Calvin said, the words hardly more than breaths. He aimed his gaze in the direction he wanted Hugh to look.

Still nothing.

"That hemlock."

Hugh saw the one Calvin indicated, the one with the spruce branches propped horizontally in front of it, like a fence.

"Trout."

Hugh stared at the spot and then he saw the silver glints

110

of fish skin behind the fence branches. Without Calvin he wouldn't have seen them.

"They're drying fish," Calvin whispered.

"Are they here?"

Calvin shook his head. Then he slid back down the boulder. "Come on." Still quiet.

"Where?"

"I know another one."

Hugh followed him as they circled far around the camp, drawing away, leaving no trace. Calvin made sure of it. Three times he stopped to study their steps. Once he walked behind Hugh, picked up a fallen twig with needles so a fresh break wouldn't be noticed on a trunk, and brushed Hugh's footprint out of a sandy underlay Hugh hadn't stepped over. He said nothing about it and never looked at Hugh.

They hiked up a steep incline to another ridge. Calvin kept twisting in and out of the trees, changing directions like wormholes. Calvin kept looking back over his shoulder. That made Hugh feel uneasy, followed. Why look back for Eric when Eric wouldn't let himself be seen in a hundred years? Not once did Calvin meet Hugh's eyes. But then Calvin was doing in the woods what Hugh should have figured out before this: he was remembering landmarks and angles of the terrain for returning. The woods showed themselves differently going one way than the reverse.

They hiked another hour. Hugh felt it in his legs. Downhill was hard on the knees. The sun was high enough now to slant shafts through the high timber. The summit fog was gone, at least over these ridges. In the unpredictable White Mountains, however, that didn't mean the other peaks were free and clear.

As they approached the other camp, Hugh felt trained to do what they had done before. When the wind didn't blow and the creatures were still, the slightest crack in the silence broadcast an intruding presence.

Again, Calvin had to show Hugh where the lean-to camp was hidden, disguised from city eyes. The camp melded into the landscape again, and again trout were drying for food in a concealed but open-air corral scarcely visible.

The two of them studied the scene from a far bank of rocks, and once more Hugh felt his reliance on Calvin's piercing gaze.

Hugh turned finally and looked to him for the answer.

Calvin shook his head.

He knew, but how?

Calvin lifted the flat of his hand. "Wait."

The silence didn't last long. A crow flew overhead, cawing into the trees below. They looked up and saw it flapping through a break in the treetops. Wing beats every two seconds, Hugh remembered from his Peterson or something. Then another caw sounded up the mountain slope where the sunlight funneled down, and another one to the right where the ridgetops blocked out the true horizon.

Calvin turned back to the camp and stared at it. Not a muscle flinched, but this time his eyes didn't examine the sweep of the scene as before. He just stared at it.

Then he stood up and said, "Come on."

Hugh followed him as he stepped fast over the same ground they had come, retracing the distance faster than arriving. Retreating. Exposed.

The cawing was Eric and Amy, all right.

Calvin walked with the end of the hunt in his stride. Saying nothing.

14

STOLEN SWEETS ARE BEST.
—COLLEY CIBBER

ZETA RAN LIKE a banshee toward Hugh and Calvin as soon as they appeared down the road from the house. Arms churning, legs galloping. Her hand raised high, she looked like a wizened old back-country Statue of Liberty on a run. "They're stealing it," she shouted, "they're stealing it!"

Her voice screeched into the trees.

Hugh and Calvin kept walking toward her till her frantic look and shouts quickened their pace. She came clamoring toward them as if she were going to steamroll right over them.

"They're stealing it!" she repeated and came to a stop, lungs bellowing, eyes white. "Right out of that house! They're stealing it!"

Calvin stared at her, waiting for her to make sense.

She grabbed Hugh's sleeve. "My high chest! They're stealing it right out of the house!" She stared at him—anybody—to do something.

"What, Zeta?"

"My high chest! My high chest!"

"How do you know?"

"I heard it on the monitor. Toop heard it. We both heard it. They're stealing it right out of that house. Right out in plain daylight. I'll kill them!"

The first thing Hugh saw when he turned into the

113

Cooper drive was Chief Maddox's blue and white. Then he saw the high chest standing on the front porch looking totally out of place. He slammed on the brakes, skidded up dust behind him, and got out of the car fast. The chief, Sarah, and Miles faced him on ground level at the base of the steps as he hurried to their midst.

"I just heard," Hugh said, glancing at the high chest, which rested on a sturdy dolly with a carrying belt wrapped around the middle drawer.

"Hugh," Sarah said, her hand at her breast, "I'm so glad to see you. That man was taking it out of the *front* door. I just didn't know what to think." Her breath heaved in and out, rekindling the shock for Hugh.

Miles hefted up the shotgun in his hand. "I almost got him! I almost blasted him to kingdom come."

"You put that down," Sarah shouted at him, "you crazy loon. You could have ruined that chest. Did you ever think of that?"

"He was stealing it, Mother, right under your nose."

"You could have ruined it!"

"It would have been in the truck," Miles said and shouldered the gun toward the long driveway.

"You put that gun down," Sarah said, "and quit thinking about yourself!"

The chief inhaled and said, "That's a good idea, Miles."

"I was thinking about your Dunlap," Miles said, ignoring the chief but putting the shotgun to his side.

Sarah tucked her lips in tight and shook her head, her eyes hot on Miles.

"What happened, Sarah?" Hugh asked.

She got a call from the post office, she told him, and she had to ask who it was because she didn't recognize the voice. He said he was a new temporary and that two large perishable boxes just came in and would she like to come into town and get them. You didn't know how long a perishable package could last, he said. Well, of course, she

114

said she'd go right in. And then he said that the packages were pretty big and heavy and would Miles come in too to help. He said she probably couldn't lift them herself. She thought nothing at the time about this new temporary knowing about Miles and never thought to ask. After all, it was the post office.

Sarah got into her car and honked for Miles to come out of that barn of his and come help her at the post office, but Miles Cooper just couldn't be bothered about helping his old mother—no, he just couldn't be bothered. He'd rather stick his head into that barn of his and never come out. She honked again, but Miles Cooper just ignored her and didn't even come out to say anything. Well, she wasn't about to get out of the car again and go traipsing after her inconsiderate son who'd rather stuff his barn full of junk inventions, including himself. Miles said he didn't hear the honking. But, according to Sarah, he heard the honking all right, he heard.

So Sarah drove away to the post office, hoping she could find somebody with a little heart left to help her, since even her very own son whom she fed with her own hands wouldn't lift his little finger. She drove out the drive and down the road and didn't think of it at the time, but on the way she passed a U-Haul truck going the other way. Why should she pay attention? It was just another truck, as far as she was concerned, delivering something, or somebody moving in, moving out—it was all the same with trucks coming and going all the time these days.

When she got to the post office, she didn't see any new temporary worker there, but she asked the postmaster about the packages all the same, the perishable ones, two of them, but he didn't know what she was talking about. No perishable packages had come into the post office for her—not that day—and nobody had called her about them either. He probably thought she was going crazy, like some other people she knew.

115

Anyway, the postmaster went and checked just the same, but he didn't find anything. Besides, he'd know. They both thought it was strange goings-on; nothing like that had ever happened before. Miles said it could be a federal offense, a real federal case, but Sarah said it was no federal offense to make mistakes, except for those made by selfish sons who'd rather clank around in old junky barns instead of helping their mothers pick up heavy packages that were perishable and that their mothers couldn't even lift off counters.

Then Sarah drove back straight away and when she turned into the drive she saw that same U-Haul truck backed up to the front steps. She hadn't ordered anything, and she couldn't imagine somebody sending her something she hadn't ordered. The closer she got, the clearer she saw what was going on. A man was wheeling out the high chest—in plain daylight, right there on the front porch. He was tilting it back and struggling with it, she could see, and he was going to wheel it right straight onto a ramp that was there between the porch and the back of the truck. He was *stealing* it!

She just couldn't believe it. He had broken right into the house. Of course, she hadn't locked the doors. Why would she do that? This was Longfield, don't you know? Longfield! She didn't have anything to hide. But there he was, wheeling that high chest of hers right out the front door. He knew she wasn't at home, didn't he? He was the one who made that phone call. He was just sitting there in that U-Haul truck waiting for her to drive away on a wild goose chase, getting her out of the house so he could break in.

Well, she just about had a heart attack, right there in the car, driving up to her own house and seeing that thief stealing her Dunlap high chest. It was the worst thing she'd ever seen in her life.

He saw her driving up and he looked at her and he knew

116

that he didn't have time to get it into the truck. She just didn't know what to do, she was so close to a heart attack about it. She just stopped the car right there in front and banged the horn. She honked and honked and banged the horn and thought that she scared him, all right—made him afraid that somebody would hear even way out here in the country. And he knew that Miles hadn't gone with her the way he was supposed to. (See, Miles said, he'd done the right thing. Besides, he hadn't heard her honking.)

Sarah honked so much that the man got so scared he put the chest down and jumped off the porch. Then Miles finally, *finally*, heard her honking and came outside his precious little barn and saw the man who had tried to take the high chest.

By the time Miles got the shotgun out of that dirty old barn of his, the man was in the front of the truck starting it up and speeding right on past Sarah. She was still honking the horn at him, but she saw who it was, all right. And then Miles took that crazy shotgun and ran down the drive after the truck. It was a crazy thing to do, running after that truck with the shotgun bouncing up and down, it near killed him, and Sarah didn't mean the robber either. Miles was running with that shotgun stuck at his shoulder, only it was jiggling and moving all over the place, scared her to death. And then he called out for that robber thief to stop and come back, which was a crazy thing to do because he wasn't going to stop and come back just because Miles Cooper said so, was he? Of course not.

So Miles kept on running and shouting and then the shotgun goes off, and that nearly scared her to death again, this great big blast and Miles going tumbling down like a baby goat and the shotgun falling out of his hands and Miles sprawling out on the road with dust puffing up all over him. Sarah thought he was dead, except that he was down there untangling his arms and legs.

Then Sarah saw Miles stand up, get the shotgun, and

blast another shot at the truck, which by this time was out the drive and on the road to town, only Miles Cooper had to shoot again, but it looked like the barrel jerked up and Miles was shooting at the clouds, just like the first time.

Sarah called for Miles to stop and get on back to the house. Then she rushed up the steps and past the high chest still standing there waiting to be stolen and called the chief, and it went out over the radio and everybody in the White Mountains knew about it.

Yes, yes, yes, Sarah recognized who it was. He drove right on past the very old woman he was robbing. Right past her. He had those same big bushy eyebrows. He was the same man who had tried to sweet-talk her the day before. The green-shirt man.

"We have the highways watched," the chief said to Hugh, corroborating the obvious first play. "North and south. And the Kacamagus Highway cutting across to the east."

"He probably dumped the truck when he got to his car," Hugh said. "It'll show up fast. You can trace a little from that."

"I almost had him, you know," Miles said to the two men. "It's not like mother said."

"Oh, you crazy loon," Sarah said, shaking her head, her eyes exasperated. "You could have killed the whole county with that shotgun, and what took you so long to hear me?"

"I saved your high chest, didn't I?" he said, wagging his hand at the porch. "See, there it is. Right there."

"You did no such thing," Sarah said. "It's a wonder *you* don't have bushy eyebrows."

"Proctor," Hugh said, back at his cabin, where he dug out the license number he'd written down—381, Massachusetts. "What do you know about the kind Wendall Kellor works with sometimes?"

118

"Lowlife, if that's what you're after."

"I was followed up here after I left Kellor. I wasn't sure at first. Now I am." Hugh gave him the lead numbers of the license on the Oldsmobile.

"But you don't know who it is."

"Right. What do you know about it?"

"I know where to find out. You've got at least something on him?"

"Darkish. Bushy eyebrows."

"Go on."

"That's it. You know that Dunlap high chest? He tried to steal it. The same one I told Kellor about."

"And you were followed from Kellor's place."

"What can you find in a hurry?"

"The quicker you hang up, the quicker I can get back."

Jean let the door slam, and Hugh heard it. He watched her walk across the lawn that was littered again with fall leaves. He met her halfway. She smiled, but it was the kind of smile with a message attached.

"Asa was here," she said, "just before you came. He has a message for you from Eric. He says to come see him sometime."

"He didn't say what he wanted, exactly?"

"No."

Hugh paused and then decided to tell her. "I was with Calvin this morning trying to find Amy."

"Did you find her?" she asked, her eyes showing hope.

He shook his head. "A lot's happened."

"I know. Somebody called me about Sarah and what happened over there. What's going on, Hugh?"

"I'm not sure yet. Asa didn't hint anything?"

"Nothing. I was shocked to hear about it. I mean, breaking into somebody's house around here. I've lived alone for five years here and I never lock my door. It's an insult to people to lock your door."

119

Hugh nodded. "Like you don't trust them."

"And then for somebody to actually break in."

"I know, it's the part of progress that people forget."

The phone rang in his cabin. He shrugged regret and ran to answer it.

"Frank Ritter," Proctor said. "I had O'Dell downtown run a check on the license."

"Does O'Dell know the guy?"

"He knows him. They call him Ritter the Runt. He's for hire. Never works for himself."

"Any connection with Kellor?"

"They think so, but they can't pin it. They know him from other enterprises, like five or six years ago the Runt burned down an abandoned tire warehouse in Milton, only he didn't know that some kids were in there using it for doping up and mattress banging, if you get my meaning. They were too doped up to get out. They burned up with the rest of the building."

"Nice."

"The police nabbed him and Ritter squawked about his friendly downtown landlord arsonist. They slammed the slumlord in for twenty years. Ritter got two years or so, because he talked. It was supposed to be an even trade, but the lawyers and the D.A. don't sweep up the ashes. You're in the rot half now, Quint."

"What else?"

"He grew up in Bartlett, New Hampshire. That's in the White Mountains, in case you've forgotten."

"Right, I know," Hugh said, adding—and meaning it—"Thanks."

"He thanks me for rot."

15

DRAGONS HAVE TO BE KILLED.
—JOHN BERRYMAN

HUGH DROVE TO Asa's to see him and hook up with Eric.
Let big Chief Maddox take care of Bushy Eyebrows Ritter,
the Runt. Sooner or later they'd find the U-Haul truck
stashed on a back dirt road or abandoned behind a
warehouse, and maybe they'd find him too, depending on
how professional a punk he was.

Then, oh, holy Judas, three miles down the road—there
it was.

At first Hugh thought he'd created Ritter out of thin air
by thinking about him. But there the thug was, not in the
Olds Hugh had seen him in when the runt had trailed him
from Wellesley, but in a blue Toyota heading north.

Hugh did what he shouldn't have. He slammed on his
brakes, whipped the wheel, and U-turned with a screech.
You stupid shit, he cursed, no wonder you're an ex-cop.
You gave yourself away, you mush-brained baboon.

The Toyota puffed out a trail of exhaust and sped off. By
the time Hugh had spun his Audi around and floored the
accelerator to China, Bushy Eyebrows was half a mile flat
out away, curving around a two-lane bend and disappearing behind a line of fat hemlocks.

Past the hemlocks the road kept curving. Hugh squealed
the Audi loud and hard, kicking dust from the shoulder,
barely missing a black Ford turning into a farmhouse
driveway. The Toyota was out of sight, somewhere on

121

another curve. When Hugh finally saw it, Ritter was heading straight for Route 3. Smart. He was going to lose himself in the crowd.

Route 3 was a coagulated artery through Franconia Notch, a narrow pass traversing the western half of the White Mountain Range. Environmentalists had fought the interstating of this highway, claiming that any widening of the road would topple the cliffs onto the traffic. The environmentalists should have let the bulldozers go and rejoiced over the blockage of the pass. As it was, tourist traffic turned the notch into arteriosclerosis of the Whites, perfect for Ritter racing in and out of the cruising leaf-peepers.

Hugh kept the blue Toyota in sight as he squirmed his Audi through the thick stream of cars. When he got blocked by left-turners, he slammed his palm on the horn and burned rubber as he squealed the tires around the pokey cars, only to jam on the brakes at another barricade of gawking tourists.

Ritter was doing the same; only he, being the hunted, was doing it faster, stretching the distance. He hit a section of the highway with a wide enough shoulder to speed ahead on the right of the traffic. Another maverick driver behind Hugh was doing the same. Once someone broke the law the rest of America followed.

Hugh saw the runt getting away. Hugh's grip on the steering wheel whitened his fingers and knuckles, but the runt had nowhere to go until he made it through the notch.

Ritter turned into the Flume parking lot. Smart again. By the time Hugh had skidded to a stop, Ritter was out of the Toyota and running toward the ticket gate and turnstiles.

Hugh wasn't going to let the runt squirm away this time. It would cost him time and distance, but Hugh yanked open the Toyota door and pulled the hood latch, then reached into the engine and ripped off the distributor cap.

122

He threw it somewhere—he didn't give a damn where—
and saw Ritter look over his shoulder at what he'd done.
Good. Now the runt knew he couldn't circle around to his
car.

A bearded man watching the whole scene got out of his
car and shouted, "Hey!"

Hugh shouted back "Police!" and it worked.

The parking lot was jammed with parked cars, with
others coming in and going out, clogging the entrance.
People in red plaid shirts, polyester tourist-pink pants, silver sunglasses, and beer-label sweatshirts filed through the
gift shop.

At the turnstile, two scowling ticket sellers stood outside
their gatehouses and shouted after Ritter as he ran
through the sauntering crowd. Hugh ran through the
turnstiles too, shoving and bumping people out of the way,
squeezing past a fat man and woman. A man wearing a cap
shouted at Hugh to watch the hell where he was going and
to get back and pay like everyone else.

Hugh shouted to the gatekeepers, "Call security!"

The Flume was a geological freak of a compact, split-
mountain canyon that the earth had waited two hundred
million years for people to pay to see. For seven hundred
feet the tight, sheer-walled gorge rose ninety feet high,
narrowing to twelve feet, and this was what Ritter ran into.
He ran in frantic escape, turning to look back over his
shoulder as he jostled through the crowd, which turned
open-mouthed and alarmed at this real-life drama that had
come to their lives.

Hugh saw Ritter disappear into the black maw of the
fifty-foot covered bridge over Pemigewasset River. A
minute later he heard his own footsteps echo through but
didn't see the runt again until he ran out the other side and
over an incline.

Hugh heard the Flume gorge ahead, water splashing and
cascading down the boulder gullet. A boardwalk rose along

the left side of the gorge. That was where Ritter pulled the gun.

The squeeze of the ocher-colored misty canyon reverberated with the steep rush of boulder-banging water as a gawking line of tourists single-filed up the boardwalk in a languid stroll through the rocky miracle. The sky was already overcast, but this funnel of sheer vertical Conway granite cut the light in half and filled the gorge with thick, wet air. The walls were slippery brown and slick, with moss and water-thriving ferns and wildflowers growing out of the crevices.

Hugh wasn't going to let the runt lose him. Ritter was from Bartlett, he knew the territory, he knew the Whites. But goddamn no, he wasn't going to lose Hugh.

The two of them ran up the boardwalk, shoving people out of the way, bumping them against each other and the railing on one side, the wet vertical sluice wall canyon on the other. At the top of the boardwalk, Ritter slipped on a wet step, losing time, losing distance. Hugh stretched his long legs to two steps at a time.

Ritter turned around, aimed the gun straight down the head-bobbing row of people at the only one of them running at him, and fired.

A woman screamed at the sight of the gun, as if it were pointing straight-armed right at her forehead.

The shot thundered a signal for a psychic stampede. The high-pitched screeching of women echoed against the gorge walls. The crowd burst into chaos.

Ritter fired again.

Hugh flattened himself against the boardwalk and yelled for everyone to get down. And Ritter ran off, disappearing over the edge of the Flume ridge top.

Hugh ran up the boardwalk, but this time he couldn't two-step it. The panicked flock of humans poured its force down the boardwalk to escape the shooting madman and the horrifying blasts of gunshot. Hugh shoved and pushed to get around shouting, cow-eyed people. Then their weight and sheer numbers imploded against him, a lone salmon struggling against the torrent.

The crowd surged past him, their shoes and boots clomping like hooves down the boardwalk, the railing creaking and bending with the sudden burden of bodies. Hugh had a clear way to the top now. He ran up the steps and slipped on the same muddy one Ritter had.

The shot had introduced a new element to this chase, but, goddamn it, Hugh wasn't going to back off. He was going to collar that son-of-a-bitch runt. Still, he eased very carefully up the last few steps of the boardwalk.

Over the top finally, Hugh saw no one. The path was full of prints but only one set dug deep—Ritter's. Hugh ran after the prints till they disappeared on the hard-packed regulation state park trail.

He stopped at a junction sign. The people on top of the Flume ridge stood clustered together, huddled against the sound of gunshots they'd heard reverberate up the Flume walls and the man with the gun in his hand running past them. They stared at Hugh, another madman on the run.

One trail led to the Visitors' Center by a loop called Rim Path, the other to the Flume Path by way of the Ridge and Wildwood paths. Which one should he take?

Hugh knew that Ritter had seen him yank out the distributor cap, but the runt was no half-wit. Hugh looked at the people—half cowering, trying to figure out whether this long-legged panting man was the good guy, a CIA agent, FBI on the prowl, American flag against the pistol-packing outlaw. The good guy didn't have a gun in his hand.

A mustachioed man took the chance, pointed to the trail to the Visitors' Center, and shouted, "There!"

Hugh ran on. His chest heaved and was aching by the time he reached the long, slow grade to the bottom, where the crowd milled around the turnstiles.

Where was the runt? He could be anywhere. In the gift shop. Behind the maintenance garage. Sidestepped into the woods.

Hugh ran through the exit turnstile, bumping people out of the way, drawing hard stares and manly shouts of rebuke. The cluster of people frozen in disbelief at the far end of the parking lot was out of sync with the rest of the commotion.

Ritter was pointing and shaking his gun at a man and woman in a white car. He looked over his shoulder, saw Hugh, then pulled the man by the shirt, yanking him out of the car. The woman screamed and pushed open her door to escape.

Hugh ran through the paralyzed crowd.

Ritter started the engine, peeled the back tires into smoke, shifted forward, and peeled the tires again. The door on the passenger side swung free. It hit another car and slammed shut as Ritter squealed the stolen Mercury through the exit gate and skidded right—north—onto Route 3. He sped down the half-shoulder until it disappeared and pressed the car into the main traffic.

Hugh ran back to his Audi, fired up, and smoked his own tires out of the parking lot onto the crowded highway.

The highway funneled into Franconia Notch and traffic intensified where the Old Man of the Mountain, a forty-foot cliff profile on Cannon Mountain, coagulated with tourists. Hugh could see panic in the way Ritter swerved the Mercury back and forth, braking and bouncing the car, to get around the mass of cars. Hugh did the same. In the rear-view mirror he could see the usual follow-the-leader—a black car—adding further chaos to the congestion.

Most of the tourists turned into the parking lot to gawk at the rocky profile, symbol of the state. This was where Ritter floored the Mercury and sped away through the last escape hatch of the notch.

Hugh honked and swerved in a tight hairpin cut around

126

the left-turners and gunned the Audi through the steep, jagged cliffs on either side. Ritter was out of sight around a bend. When Hugh finally caught sight of him, the Mercury had kept on Route 3 to the east, not on the Interstate 93 hookup to Littleton. Smart again. The runt was staying in the mountains he knew.

On the top side of the Whites, Ritter swerved and tilted the Mercury around the curves and raced at full reckless speed where the road flattened out for the nine miles to Twin Mountains junction. Hugh figured the runt would turn north again, but he kept right and was heading back into the thick of the mountains, to Crawford Notch. That was it! He was heading back to hometown Bartlett, where he could lose himself.

Then, at Fabyan, a pockmark village on the highway, Ritter took a left to the Cog Railroad. A dead end. What the hell? By the time Ritter sped up the long incline to the parking lot, Hugh had lost too much distance. Minutes later, Ritter was on the old-time pot-bellied, coal-burning locomotive, the gun at the engineer's head, and going up the mountain.

The three-mile railroad had been built in 1869 as the first mountain-climbing cog railroad in the world, and it chugged up the steep incline to the top of Mt. Washington, highest peak in the Northeast, highest in the Presidential Range of the Whites, a cloud-buster in these parts.

The black puffing steam engine crept up the mountain one cog turn at a time, clawing its undergears into the holding track, pushing two bright yellow and red passenger cars ahead of it. Meanwhile, the would-be passengers remained behind, cowering at the side of the gift shop and staring bewildered and frightened at the gun-toting theft, like a stunt scene on a Western movie set turned real.

Hugh screeched his Audi to a stop, jumped out, and ran to the wire gate. The train could move only as fast as a man could climb, only easier. So he ran down the platform,

127

leaped off, and headed into the thinned-out trees that paralleled the tracks. At the base the incline was soft enough to make distance. Then the haughty mountain took permanent hold. He had to make it to the treeline before the locomotive. Otherwise, he would be a sitting duck.

Mt. Washington was a vortex of winds, a rocky bald summit that had once clocked the highest wind velocity ever recorded, over two hundred miles per hour—way over. Only now it was the fog that greeted Hugh. The mountain was smothered with fog.

He ran through the birches and maples, many of them losing their leaves and opening up the sightline. His breath heaved heavy and fast.

The train engine chugged along, then when it hit a sharp angle up, it slowed.

Ritter fired twice. Wasted shots.

Hugh passed the engine, ran sideways to a low boulder pass the train had to creep by, and jumped onto the outside iron steps of the lead passenger car in front of the tourist-cute engine.

Ritter leaned out the engine compartment and fired alongside the car. Wasted shots again. He couldn't leave the engineer to get Hugh. He couldn't wait for Hugh to get him.

Hugh kicked open the door and stomach-crawled down the aisle four feet, then rolled under the passenger seats. He waited. He crawled down the aisle again a few feet, then rolled under the seats.

The light faded, and fog enshrouded the chugging engine and cars, dampening the noise, shutting down the rest of the world.

Hugh eased up and looked.

The engineer shouted down the center of the other car: "There! Out there!"

Hugh saw the foggy silhouette of Ritter fading in a spastic rush to the netherworld, disappearing, vanished. God-damn smart, goddamn smart.

Hugh ran to the outside steps and stared into gray noth-ingness. The gurgling, ugly scream that emerged from the fog didn't make sense. A man didn't scream like that when he fell down.

Hugh jumped from the car, his sense of caution heightened by the nothingness that seemed all that was left of the world—and the disembodied, terrorized cry of what sounded like death.

Instinct halted his rush to the source of that terror. He saw only the waving, floating, gauzy grayness. The security of the bulky yellow and red train, he knew, was also being swallowed up behind. But he mustn't look back, mustn't turn his back to the scream.

He eased forward, but the dimensionless fog made his progress seem as if he were on a treadmill, getting nowhere.

Then, frighteningly close, he heard the fog-muted thud of boots on rock scampering away.

He squinted at the sound, and there, in the flash of a wave of fog, the stick figure of a fleeing human being ap-peared. The moment was brief, but it was enough to signal the approaching horror of being ambushed. Hugh froze at the anticipated pain to his gut, at the expectation of a realization that he was dying for some reason he couldn't comprehend.

Then he saw the other fog-crushed stick figure, the grotesque sprawl of a human being on the boulders, arms and legs askew, its head hanging upside down. It was a colorless phantom in the thick, wispy vapors, but the closer Hugh inched toward it, the more vivid became the shapes and colors.

Frank Ritter fixed an icy stare upward at gray eternity, his bushy eyebrows black and bold over his popping eyeballs. His neck was creased deep with a corded string tie, one of those tourist ties bought at gift shops, the kind with an emblem you push up to your throat.

This one read: "Welcome to the White Mountains."

16

SOMETHING HIDDEN. GO AND FIND IT.
GO AND LOOK BEHIND THE RANGES.
—RUDYARD KIPLING

FRANK RITTER WAS finished, but who the hell had done it? And where had he come from?

The Cog Railroad had stopped, and the silence isolated Hugh all the more in the wet air. The only way out was down, and that was easy. He walked out of the cloud like a ghost of himself, then heard the engine start up again and the cog gears clank down the loud iron tracks, the black locomotive puffing out of the smeary heavens, a deus ex machina come to rescue Hugh Quint.

He ran to the locomotive, explained to the wide-eyed, worried engineers that, no, the body shouldn't be carried down until investigators had examined the scene as is, and rode down Mt. Washington to the station and a telephone.

The state police said they'd have officers out there in four minutes and to stay there. Yes, sir, they knew who Hugh Quint was; Chief Maddox had informed them, but stay there. They'd like to talk about it. Hugh stayed.

Whoever strangled Ritter had known what he was doing, known how to operate in the fog, known the territory. But who didn't around there? Maybe Miles, who had trouble with reality let alone real estate. Eric could slick through the fog like that. So could Calvin or Toop or, for that matter, Zeta. *Is fecit cui prodest*—he who profits by crime is guilty of it.

But who could be right at the critical spot when Ritter disappeared into the fog? That was impossible for anyone to know beforehand. Hugh had been followed, all right. Of course. It was the black Ford zigzagging in and out of the traffic behind him when *he* was behind Ritter. Or maybe the guy had been following Ritter in the first place. Hugh had blown it by not remembering the license number. It was reversed in the rear-view mirror and too far away. Then he should have looked at the guy's goddamn face. Well, hell, that was also too far away, and back. Besides, Ritter had commanded all of Hugh's attention, and that was always mistake number one, side-tracking a wider focus.

Whoever it was followed the two of them to the Cog Railroad, saw what was happening, got out, and climbed through the trees just like Hugh, only he climbed farther out, unseen, silent, waiting. Hugh had made just the right moves and forced Ritter into the open terrain, into the fog. The killing had to be premeditated, and the right time worked into the killer's perfect opportunity. He had the strangling weapon ready, and it said what he wanted it to say, just like the other killings.

When Hugh called Proctor Hammond, he told his answerman about Ritter and the theory about the black Ford following him. But who was in the car? How'd he get up the mountain so fast? How'd he know when Ritter was in the fog? How'd he get away? How did it fit with the other killings? Had Kellor set Ritter up to steal the chest, or did Ritter do it on his own? Did Ritter's killer want the chest himself, or did he just want to kill Ritter for what he knew and might reveal if Hugh nabbed him?

" 'Questioning is not the mode of conversation among gentlemen,' " Proctor said, cagey as a catamount.

Hugh laughed. "*You* said that?"

"I stole it from Samuel Johnson."

"Why, Proctor, I thought you were entirely original."

"Funny. I'm laughing hysterically. I'm slapping my knee. I'm gasping for breath at this Shakespearean witticism . . .

"But, Proctor, you steal once, it's plagiarism; steal twice, it's research."

"I've heard. Good-bye."

"Who's doing all this killing up here?" Hugh asked, suddenly straight as a razor, before Proctor could hang up.

"From what you tell me"—Proctor was off and running—"you have the human genetic impulse for unadulterated barbaric greed converging from all angles on a silky chest of drawers. Human beings transmogrify into teeth-gnashing hyenas when a chest of drawers has value and will have more value. Gimmie, gimmie, gimmie. Human beings can put their treasures in shoe boxes, if a Dunlap chest has its only value as a storage box, but art destroys itself when it gets out of the hands of artists. They don't call money *filthy* lucre for nothing. Buying and selling has nothing to do with art, it has to do with buying and selling, and buying and selling has to do with greed. Greed!"

Hugh waited, picturing Proctor pacing like a puma in his whirlwind office, his eyes swiveling back and forth even faster than his head swiveling back and forth.

"Greed is after that Dunlap chest, and whoever owns it—"

"—Sarah Cooper."

" . . . is a little old lady who can be maneuvered out of it by that loony son of hers, or that thug Ritter, or anyone else up there in that outback of primitivism."

Calvin or Toop or Zeta or Asa or Eric, maybe even Amy.

"And then comes that Young Man of the Mountains."

"Very witty, Proctor."

"That Abenaki and his Woman of the Wilds. He's impelled by a greed for righteous social justice, the economic justice of a Mother Earth ethic that boils down to whoever's-first-owns-it, and he was there before John

133

Locke. Now maybe he's so greedy for the righteousness of his people, for the return of the White Mountains to his people—or the return of his people to the White Mountains—that he is maneuvering Amy to sell the chest and contribute the loot to his cause."

"She can't. Well, she could, but Sarah's will stipulates that as long as Miles doesn't sell the house Amy can keep the chest there for future security, and Miles can't sell the house if Amy still has the chest in it. Sarah says that Amy is smart enough to know that once the chest is gone she has nothing left."

"That was before she had Eric."

"Maybe."

"Besides, you talk as if you've seen the will."

"I haven't actually seen it, but I know what's in it. Sarah told me."

"Sarah told you."

"Do I detect some questioning in your gentlemanly voice?"

"Good detective, Hugh Quint, good detective."

Hugh smiled. Proctor Hammond was a vexing, accurate son of a bitch.

"Besides, killing for a cause loosens up anybody's tidy morals. Quantity of life serves quality of life—a life for a life-style. It makes no difference to these people."

"To Eric Cornplanter."

"You're the one who said it. Just look at that name. It's a name a crusader of causes would have, but nine out of ten causes create nine out of ten cretins. The world has enough cretins already. We don't need another ninety percent."

"Present company excepted, of course."

"I speak for myself, of course, but I tell you something else, Quint, and that's that a causer on the kill gladly risks exposure by making sure his killings are *known* to have something to do with the cause. Otherwise, the killings have no point. A causer captions his killings." He stopped

134

short, the silence obviously a caption to his pleasure at such a scintillating turn of phrase.

"What champion form you are in today, Proctor."

"You have such a limited view of time."

"That's because time is the anti-matter of space and therefore must be the continuum of the eternal present in order to keep space in existence by counterbalance."

"The truth of the *matter* is that time is the deterioration of space."

"Time equals the past times the future squared."

"So Einsteinian, for a philosopher. Time is the difference between the perception of space and its reality."

"Wisely spoken, Proctor."

"I know. 'Hurry up, please. It's time.'"

"Is that plagiarism or research?"

"Let's put it this way. If you opened a big jar in Nag Hammadi, Egypt, and discovered the Gnostic gospels, on one hand, you'd be stealing—once—from history. On the other hand, you'd be doing fabulous research that could change the history of the world. Guess what I'd call it. But then the world isn't ruled by literature and science. It's ruled by illiterate assassins who'd just as soon burn up a scroll of scribbly papyrus as burn down the Alexandrian Library. It makes no difference to these limbic-brained lizards. Meanwhile, the gospels were hidden in a secret jar and therefore so was the *truth*. That's what happens when . . ."

"Hey, that's it!"

"He tells me that's it," Proctor said to the urgency in Hugh's voice.

"You gave me an idea. Thanks. I should've thought about it before."

"You're welcome. Good-bye, plagiarist."

Hugh replaced the phone and thought about the possibility that Proctor, unknowingly, had cast his way. But it all depended on Sarah's Dunlap high chest.

He dialed Sarah's number. When someone drew up a will with a lawyer, the original document usually was kept away from the individual's house. This safeguarded against fraud. A survivor of the deceased could find the will in the home, read that he was not included in the distribution of the goods of the estate, and tear up the will. No one would know. If someone discovered the fraud, the crime would be extremely difficult to prove since the original will had been destroyed. This was the reason that lawyers either held the original documents in their vaults or suggested that they be placed in another safekeeping location away from the home, such as a bank safety-deposit box, although a survivor could have access to this too. Most lawyers offered their vaults for these wills as a service, no charge. A copy of the original will was then given to place somewhere accessible and known in the house, with a note attached saying where the original was held for the survivors who rummaged through the deceased's papers.

Sarah answered on the fourth ring. "Oh, Hugh!" she said. "You found Amy! Is she really all right? How is she? Is she coming back?"

He should have said something right away. "I'm sure she's all right, Sarah," he said, and then it clicked. "What do you mean is she really all right?"

"I just got a note from her. She said, 'I'm all right. We're not doing anything wrong.' That's all she said. It came through the mail."

"I was close to her, Sarah. I didn't see her, but I'm convinced she's doing fine. She's with Eric, you know."

"Oh, that Eric. Now wouldn't you think she would write me something more than this little note?"

"She wrote you that though."

"She did, the poor little mixed-up thing."

"And she hand wrote it?"

"Oh, yes," Sarah said matter-of-factly. "Oh, I see what you mean. Yes, Hugh, that's Amy's handwriting. I can tell.

She wrote the note. It's her handwriting."

"Sarah," he said, easing in, "will you please not say your next answer out loud—just answer yes or no. Is Miles there with you?"

"Now, Hugh, what are you up to?"

"Is he? Just yes or no."

"Well, yes, but what are you up to?"

"It's about that high chest of yours."

"What about it? Now what are you up to, Hugh dear?"

"I better ask you in person. Is Miles going to be around there a while?"

"Yes. But you better find out if that Jean can cook you a good soup first, Hugh dear."

Good old Sarah. "Can you get Miles to go someplace so we can talk?"

"I don't know what you have in mind, Hugh dear, but yes, I think that's a good idea. I can do that. That'll be easy as pie."

17

TRUST NOT HIM WITH YOUR SECRETS, WHO, WHEN LEFT
ALONE IN YOUR ROOM, TURNS OVER YOUR PAPERS.
—JOHANNA KASPAR LAVATER

SARAH'S AROMATIC KITCHEN filled the rest of the house with
her nose-twitching, up-country beef stew simmering and
steaming on the stove. The French may have their cas-
soulet, but Americans had Sarah's stew.

"See," she said, wiping her hands on the underside of
her apron, "here's what Amy wrote. 'I'm all right. We're
not doing anything wrong.' Now why would she say that
she's not doing anything wrong? Of course, she's not doing
anything wrong. But that Eric. Now he shouldn't be kidnapping her like that."

"Well, we have to find out if he really is kidnapping her.
I don't think he is. You don't either, do you?"

"I don't know what to think. All I know, Hugh, is that I
don't know what *you're* up to. What are you up to?"

Hugh glanced around and lowered his voice. "Is Miles
here?"

"I chased him over to the store to get me some fresh
sweet cream. Just like you told me, Hugh dear."

"It's just that I wanted to ask you something in private."

"I know. And I told that Miles of mine that if he wanted
to eat anything ever again in this house to get down to the
village and bring me back some fresh sweet cream. I said, if
you want to eat another meal here don't you go getting
yourself lost in that cluttered-up old barn either." She

leaned toward Hugh and grinned. "I knew that he'd come running over here if he wasn't off the premises when you came. That boy." She clicked her tongue and shook her head. "Now, Hugh, what did you want to know?"

"Sarah," he said, letting her grandmotherly smile of permission erase his feeling of intrusion, "I know that it was a shock to have your high chest almost stolen right from your own front porch, and you'll find out pretty soon about the man who tried to steal it, but I have an idea that the chest might have a secret compartment. A lot of those old ones do."

She stared straight at him, not flinching, a smile on her grandmotherly face.

When she didn't answer, he asked it straight out. "Does it?"

It gave her time to think. "It does," she said. "Of course, it does." She paused, thinking more. "Do you want to see it?"

Hugh nodded.

She led the way to the glorious maple-wood Dunlap creation standing in its presiding way against the showcase wall in the front room. She stood on her tiptoes, stretched up to the one-third-wide drawer on the top left-hand side, removed it, and handed it to Hugh. Then she reached into the chest and pressed her index finger up against the inside panel somewhere next to the partition to the central small drawer. Directly above the center drawer and below the scallop carving on the bonnet, a thin, flat panel sprung open.

Sarah turned and smiled at Hugh. "Now isn't that clever? No one would ever know just looking at it, would they?"

"Not in a hundred years."

"It's two hundred years old, Hugh dear."

He smiled back and said, "What do you keep in there?"

"My will, Hugh dear."

"Ah, you do. Now correct me if I'm wrong, but in your will you say that Miles can't sell the house if Amy still has this high chest in here, which you're giving to her. Is that right?"

"No, Hugh dear."

"It isn't?"

"Miles told you that, didn't he?"

"Yes."

"That's what I wanted him to tell you. In fact, he can tell everybody else that too. And he has. For all I know, the whole town thinks that."

"I don't understand, Sarah."

She reached up and removed the white envelope with the will in it. "I told Miles about the will, and Amy too, but I never really showed it to them. What I said and what this says may be a little tiny bit different." She smiled and waited for Hugh to ask the obvious.

"What does it say?"

"It says that when I die—and I will, don't you forget that, Hugh—the high chest is to be returned to Zeta and Toop Tucker, that's what it says."

Hugh stared back at the smiling old woman. "Returned? You want the high chest returned?"

She nodded, smiling. "I do," she said, opening the envelope and removing a slip of paper. "And here's the bill of sale for it too. I want that returned right along with the high chest. People don't know about this bill of sale, but that's what it is. Bryan, poor Bryan, gave it to me a little while ago. He said I should have it here. Of course, he kept the original will in his vault."

"But why did you tell Miles and Amy something different?"

"You know Miles, that scalawag son of mine. He'd trick Amy, I know it, just to get this high chest and sell it all for himself. This way Miles and Amy have to work together, they have to stay together. They have to need each other."

"And after you're gone?"

"They'll just have to work it out, but at least they've been together all this time."

"You're really something, Sarah."

"I know," she said, mischievous eyes sparkling. "I don't just bake bread all the time, you know."

"But to give the chest back after all these years?"

"Oh, I know what Zeta calls me, and maybe it's true, but something fine as this high chest is too nice to have been won in a silly poker game. It's just *wrong*, but one thing led to another over the years, and when Eddie died I almost gave it back. Then I saw the bickering between Miles and Amy, and I came to the conclusion that, for now, keeping them needing each other was more important to me than this old chest was to the Tuckers."

"That's why you hid the will?"

"It sure is. If I told Miles where the copy was, he'd sneak in there and read it all himself, wouldn't he? Of course, he would, and find out the truth. He doesn't know about this secret compartment."

Hugh looked her straight in the eye. "Somebody is killing for this chest."

"I know that."

"Will you help me find out who?"

She nodded.

"No matter who it ends up to be?"

"Hugh dear, I'm tougher than you think."

"It might be dangerous."

"I hope so."

"And it might not work."

"But it might."

He smiled, and told her his scheme.

The next morning Miles called Hugh faster than the sun rose.

"You know what Mother is going to do?" he shouted

through the wires. "She's going to put the high chest into *storage*! Can you believe that? Into *storage*! Hey, I heard you killed that Ritter guy, the guy who was stealing the chest."

"Judas, Miles you got it wrong."

"Well, it was something like that. What's the difference?"

"There's plenty of difference. And it's too damn early to think about it."

If Miles didn't need a leash, he needed at least some additional cogs in his cranium to keep him on track.

Miles had returned home with the fresh sweet cream and Sarah had told him about putting the chest in storage. That must have been a gripping scene.

"You've got to tell her not to do it!" Miles shouted into the phone, his voice desperate for salvation.

"You tell her, Miles. She's your mother."

"She won't listen to me. I don't know *why* she won't listen to me. What about Amy? She hasn't even asked Amy about it."

"It's your mother's high chest, Miles."

"It's going to be Amy's, so she should know about this. Besides, that Ritter guy almost stole it right out of the house. If it hadn't been for me coming along, he *would've* stolen it."

"That's not how I remember it."

"You killed him, that's why. Up there in the fog where nobody could see."

"Come on, Miles."

"Well, I didn't kill him. She's going to put the chest in *storage* tomorrow. Tomorrow!"

"She has her reasons."

"Because it was almost stolen, that's what she says anyway. If I hadn't come along ..." Miles paused for Hugh's reaction and, getting none, continued. "She doesn't want it stolen again."

"Can you blame her?"

"Hell, yes, but she won't listen to me. She listens to *you*, and you're nobody."

142

"Uh-huh."

"Well, you're not her only *son*."

"Miles, I've got to go. Besides, you're driving me nuts."

"Who's driving you nuts? Where you going?"

"I've got to see Eric."

"Eric! You're going to kill him too?"

Hugh hung up and stared out the window. He stared at Jean's window. He stared at it until that old devil instinct conjured those early-morning, fleeting, filmy, sumptuous fantasies of silky auburn hair veiling long naked neck and shoulders—the soft friendly enclaves of a welcoming woman, curves and smiles and arms and legs. Woman of the Healing Heart, Woman of Deep Sleepy Eyes, all open and waiting, waiting.

Why wait? Why the hell wait?

He opened his door and walked straight to hers. Be there, Jean Gerard. Be awake.

Miles Cooper could drive anybody nuts.

And Hugh Quint could be dead in twenty-four hours.

"Gather ye rosebuds while ye may. Old Time is still aflying."

No answer. She's still asleep. Good. This is absurd.

Time to go.

"Hi," she said, opening the door—*awake*—her blue painter shirt unbuttonned—all open—over her cream-colored turtleneck, her face signaling that only Hugh Quint could possibly generate such a receptive response at being interrupted from the only other consuming entity in her life—painting.

He couldn't say anything. He managed a smile. He walked inside.

Do women know so *much*?

He said, "How would you like me to make love with you?"

She said, smiling, "I'd like it."

"No, I mean *how*." What an idiotic thing to say.

"How?"

143

Of course, she had to ask that. "I mean, what can I do to make love with you?" Another idiotic thing to say. What an idiot.

She said, "Well, we could close the door." And then she closed it.

"Good idea."

"Now, where were we?"

She came to him and wrapped her arms around his waist. And all the time he'd thought this was going to be a bumbling unilateral declaration of desire.

"We were listening to some man getting it all wrong about his lust for this beautiful woman in my arms," he said. "He doesn't speak the language too well."

"What language is that?" She leaned back to see him better and her hips moved into his.

He smiled. "Body English."

"Bawdy English?"

He laughed.

"I think he does very well, actually. He makes his point, considering the circumstances."

"Such a forgiving beauty he has in his arms."

He leaned to her neck. He kissed her up and down as she eased her head back in a slow dreamy arc until he was kissing the front hollow of her throat, pulsing from the light skim of his lips. He moved his kisses to her cheek and then slowly to her lips, soft and ripe, supremely ready.

He let her loose a moment and smiled once more.

"Considering the circumstances," he echoed.

"What circumstances?"

He reached under her shirt and pulled out the back of her turtleneck, then slid his flat palms up the full length of her back, cupping his fingers over her shoulders, forcing himself tighter against her.

"These circumstances," he answered.

"Oh, those. I thought you were talking about the world at large."

144

"Don't remind me. I only want to think about these circumstances right here, and how much I am liking these circumstances."

"Ummm. Me too," she said, and they kissed again.

18

WE LOVE TOO MUCH, HATE IN THE SAME EXTREME.

—HOMER

No DOUBT ABOUT it. Hugh came away from Jean's cabin a jubilant man. He got in his Audi and drove the back road to the shadowy entrance to Asa Nickerson's place. He parked the car and hiked up the path.

By the time he reached the clearing with Asa's cabin facing that vast long panorama of the White Mountains, Hugh's jubilance had been subdued. He was feeling watched and wary. The slightest scrape of one leaning spruce against another perked his ears. Nature or Eric Cornplanter? The scamper of chipmunks and their high-pitched chitter chatter? Real or signal calls? What about the crows he could hear but not see? Or the squawking blue jays? He wasn't any match for the Abenaki, or even Asa, for that matter. Maybe Asa was following him this time. Maybe the faint distant muffled sounds up in the piney dark were those of Asa practicing again on Hugh— private target, easy mark.

Nope. There sat the old hairy loner on his front cabin steps, leaning his elbows on his knees, looking straight on at Hugh as if he had heard the long-legged, lanky lad heading his way the day before, and had been waiting on the steps ever since. The silence of the woods had taught this old man that city silence was a different breed altogether. From the way he crouched and studied what was approaching, it was clear that he preferred the woods.

146

"Asa."

"You got the message."

"Yes, Jean said Eric wanted to see me." Which was perfect because now Hugh wanted to see Eric.

Asa smiled and nodded and stood up in a slow motion, saying, at about the same speed, "He'll be around."

That either meant Eric was there already someplace hidden, or Hugh would have to wait a few hours. Asa Nickerson had reached the stage of life at which interpretation was left to others.

Hugh shifted on his feet and turned around as casually as he could.

"He'll be here."

"Asa, tell me about Amy."

"She's all right."

"Have you seen her?"

He nodded. "She's fine. She's with Eric, that's all. Give her time."

"Nobody else has seen her."

"Probably won't either, for a spell."

Asa stepped to the edge of the clearing and faced the woods that slanted up the mountainside. He bent his neck back, opened his mouth, and cawed out the cry of the crow in short screechy bursts. The caws sounded into the maze of timber and cliffs. He waited motionless, staring into the trees.

Finally, distant caws sounded back in return through the same woods and granite. Asa looked over his shoulder and walked back to his perch on the porch.

When Eric appeared ten minutes later, he was behind Hugh, not from the direction of the crow caws. Hugh knew because Asa nodded in his slow way toward Eric, who had approached without the slightest rustle of wind.

The Abenaki wore the same clothes that blended into the woods, and the same intense face and unwavering eyes.

The three of them waited in a triangle of silence a few

147

moments. Then Eric Cornplanter, the Abenaki, the caw of the crow, said without any preliminaries, "I know Calvin and you tried to find me. I know about Calvin and I know about you. I know what you're after, and I know what Calvin is trying to do."

"Eric," Hugh said, "I want to see Amy."

"She'll see you when she wants to see you."

"Is she here someplace?"

"You won't find her."

"Just like Calvin didn't find you?"

"Calvin can never find me, and he can never find Moonseed as long as she's with me. He wants her, and he's blaming me for these killings."

"Is he?"

The hardness glazed over Eric's eyes. "These mountains belong to my people and Moonseed's people, and Calvin is not of them. He wants Moonseed, and I want these mountains for my people. I know about these killings, and I know Calvin wants me blamed and out of the way. Calvin cannot find me and Moonseed, and so he wants the white man's law to find me and kill me. *Nobody* can find me unless I want them to. Nobody."

"That's probably true."

"I watched you and Calvin at our camps. I saw you before you saw our camps, you and Calvin with his rifle. I followed you. I watched you. I saw what you were doing. I know what you're doing. I saw you wait at the camps, and then I let Calvin know that I saw him. Calvin wants Moonseed, and he can never have her. She is no longer Amy. She is Moonseed."

"Sarah wants Amy, her daughter."

"Moonseed is daughter of these mountains."

"Amy is part of Sarah's will. She—"

"I know all about the will," Eric said, cutting Hugh off. "I know about the chest and I know about the house. I know about her brother—her stepbrother—and these things mean nothing to her."

148

"What do they mean to you?"

Eric said nothing. Then: "The chest is a tool. If it is Moonseed's, it is for her to decide what to do with it."

"Is there anything you wouldn't do to get these mountains back to your people, Eric?"

"Nothing."

Hugh stared back, wondering whether the answer was bravado or the fearless truth. He let Eric's answer include murder and theft, conspiracy to defraud and grand larceny.

"Nothing is more important than the return of my people," Eric said, the flare in his eyes matching his words. "The Great Spirit of these mountains is with me and helps me and guides me. What I do is what must be done. What I have yet to do must be done. Moonseed will help me. She will do what must be done for our people. She is with me. I am with her. What I have is hers. What she has is mine. This piece of furniture of hers—"

"It's still Sarah's," Hugh corrected.

Eric cut himself short.

"Well," Hugh said, suddenly casual, suddenly aware that this was the time to say it, "Sarah's going to lock up that high chest in storage someplace anyway. Tomorrow."

Toop and Zeta were splitting and stacking wood when Hugh drove up. Toop glanced over his shoulder, grabbed the long-handled ax with both big hands, arched the shiny blade over his back, and whacked the log in two. Zeta gathered up the two chunks and banged them down on the rest of the cordwood under the woodshed. Then the two of them turned full-face to Hugh, who was getting out of his car and coming toward them.

"Well, well," Zeta said, "Mr. Private Detective. Out here investigating the falling leaves. Seeing how many bodies they're covering up!" She gave forth one of her high screechy laughs.

"Just keep on stacking, will you, woman?" Toop said

149

and placed another log on the chopping block.

"Hold your horses, and say hello to Mr. Detective here. He came out here to see you."

"He didn't come out here to see me. Besides, I didn't hear *you* saying hello." Toop gripped the ax tight and whacked the log in two like a hot knife through butter. Then he turned and allowed himself the effort. "What brings you out here?"

"Toop. Zeta. How are you? Actually, I was wondering if Calvin was around."

"Calvin ain't around," Toop said, positioning another log on the block. "Come on, woman. Stack 'em up."

"I'm gettin' to it. Keep your shirt on. You ain't the only one in the world, you know." She picked up the logs and heaved them onto the other cordwood. "Calvin's always around."

"But not around here," Toop said and split the log with another two-handed blast of power.

"What you want him for?" Zeta asked, her needle-eye look stitching her thready mouth shut tighter than bark on a sapling.

"I'm still looking for Amy, and I was just wondering if he had heard anything lately, or had seen her."

"Mr. Private Detective sure wonders a lot," she said. "Wondering this, wondering that. Maybe he ought to wonder who's stabbing lawyers in the back and hanging neighbors by the neck until they're deader than a doornail right down that road there. And what about that strangulation up there on Mt. Washington? You was right there, right there next to him. That's what I heard. Makes *me* wonder about some things."

"Woman, leave the man alone. Get stacking, will you?"

"I'm stacking, when I want to stack," she said, and picked up the logs, heaving them onto the others. "I heard about that mountain killing and nobody does that lest he knows these mountains. I know that much."

150

"Who doesn't know these mountains," Toop said just before he axed another log in two.

The blade thudded into the block. He wagged the handle and yanked the ax free.

"The difference is, I know somebody who *wants* these mountains," Zeta said, glaring squint-eyed from under her eyebrows.

"Gossip monger," Toop said under his breath as he whacked another log in two.

"I heard that!" Zeta shouted. "I heard what you called me!"

"I don't care what you heard."

"Calvin's looking for that Indian and he's going to find him, too."

"Calvin can take care of himself," Toop shot back at her. "Just leave him be and quit telling him about Amy."

"I'll tell him about Amy if I want to, Mr. *Gambling* Man. You want me to put my neck right there on that block, don't you?"

"I'll take care of anybody who wants to put her neck right down there on that block, you betcha. You want to put your neck down there?"

"You're a gambling man. You put *your* neck down there and see what I can do."

"Just pick up those logs and *stack* 'em, woman."

"I'll pick them up when I want to," Zeta shouted, and picked up the logs and stacked them, loudly.

"Well," Hugh said, shifting on his feet, pausing, looking over at the paint-peeling house. "I just wanted to rest Sarah's mind about Amy."

Toop went back to chopping the logs. Zeta said, "Ol' Mrs. Proper ought to rest my mind about that Tucker high chest. She ought to do that first, if you ask me."

Toop whacked a neck-size log and said, "Nobody's asking you."

"Nobody's talking to you." Then to Hugh: "It was almost

151

stolen right out from under her high nose besides. That's the Tucker chest and it was almost stolen!" She whipped up her arm and pointed down the road. "There's Calvin!"

Calvin stepped in his mechanical way down the wheel-rutted road with the brown grass and needles lying on the center ridge. The rifle he carried swung with his right arm. From a distance it was easy to see Zeta's tight-eyed face in his. The three of them watched as Calvin approached with the inbred wariness he showed to everyone, even his parents. Zeta was the first to say anything to him.

"Mr. Detective Man came to see you. Wants to know about Amy."

Calvin stopped, the rifle tilted toward the ground at Hugh's feet. He kept his eyes on Hugh's, as if Toop and Zeta weren't there.

"What about her?"

"Have you had any luck finding Amy?" Hugh asked.

Calvin stared back. "It ain't luck."

"He'll find her," Zeta said, reaching up and patting her mountain son on the back. "Won't you?"

"I know where their camps are," he said without a twitch of acknowledgement of Zeta.

"See?" she said.

Toop whacked another log in two.

"Calvin and Amy grew up together, you know," Zeta said. "They belong together and Calvin's going to get them together too. That Indian kidnapped her, that's what he did, and Calvin isn't going to let him get away with it neither, are you, Calvin?"

"She's half Indian herself," Toop growled, kicking the split logs away. "Are you going to stack these, woman, or what?"

"I'll stack them when I want to stack them," she snapped, and this time she let the logs lie. "I know one thing, Mr. Gambling Man. Calvin's going to get Amy back before you get that high chest back. That's what I know as sure as standing here watching you chop off my head a hundred times a day!"

"Calvin," Hugh said, priming the tinder, "do you think Eric kidnapped Amy?"

"Sure, he kidnapped her," Zeta shouted.

Toop slammed another log upright on the block. "He wasn't asking you."

"Well, I'm telling him."

Toop whacked the log in two and kicked the halves away.

Calvin studied Hugh and said, "She doesn't belong with him. He's crazy. He drugged her or something. She doesn't know what she's doing. He's telling her lies and she believes him because she's out there and can't get away."

Hugh saw Calvin fight the heat surfacing inside, the shivering of anger around his eyes, the tightened grip on the rifle, the quavering words sounding from his hard throat.

"Amy sent Sarah a note and said she was all right," Hugh said.

"With that Indian?" Zeta shouted.

"I'll find her," Calvin said, ignoring her, staring at Hugh. "He's got her drugged. She doesn't belong with him. He's crazy."

"She belongs with Calvin," Zeta said, patting his back. "Who knows what that crazy Indian is doing up there?"

"Maybe you ought to back off a while," Hugh said. "Let things cool off."

Calvin stared at him.

"Calvin'll do what he wants to do," Toop said, defending his bloodline.

Hugh nodded. "I suspect so," he said. Then he got to what he wanted to get to. "Well, I've got to go help Sarah with the high chest."

"You go do that for ol' Mrs. Proper," Zeta said. "Do what?"

153

Perfect. "She doesn't want the high chest stolen so she's putting it into storage someplace. Tomorrow."

19

FOR THE LION CANNOT PROTECT HIMSELF FROM TRAPS.
—MACHIAVELLI

THAT NIGHT HUGH ate dinner with Sarah and Miles, and immediately after the last spoonful of butter-bubbling apple crisp, Sarah shooed them out of the house.

"Go on, you two," she said. "Leave an old woman to herself. It's time to go. Go on, go on. I want some peace and quiet, and that means you, Miles."

"Me?" he protested. "What about Hugh? What about *him*?"

She got up from her chair and went around the table, shooing Miles away with flicks of her fingers. "He's going too. Both of you."

"Sarah, let us help with the dishes," Hugh said, standing up.

"Next time, Hugh dear. Tonight I just want to clean up and go to bed. Now off you two go. I'm a sound sleeper once I get started, but I can't get started with two men around here, especially you, Miles. You make so much *noise* all the time."

"I do not!"

"Miles," she shouted. "You wait right there." She went into the kitchen.

"Come on out to the barn," Miles whispered. "I got something to show you, something fantastic."

"Tomorrow," Hugh said. "I've got to check something out."

"But it's fantastic. I mean, it is fan*tas*tic."

"Yeah, right."

"It *is*."

"Miles," Sarah said as she came through the doorway, "you go fix this and don't come back until you do."

"I don't fix coffeepots," he said, insulted.

"You fix this coffeepot, Miles, or you won't be eating any more of anything in this house, you hear me? I like my coffee in the morning, and that means you just better fix it tonight or Miles Cooper is going to be in real trouble. Real trouble."

"But I don't fix coffeepots."

"You told me you fixed anything, so go do it."

He took the pot and glared at it.

"Now off with you," she said, shooing them out the screen door onto the porch.

"Come on out to the barn," Miles said to Hugh.

"Miles! Hugh is trying to find Amy and investigate all these killings and everything! You leave him be and go out there and fix that coffeepot tonight or don't show your face in my kitchen ever again, you hear me?"

Miles's mouth drooped and he stared daggers at her. Then, with the theatrics of sympathy he had mastered so well, he turned and walked away slumped-shouldered to his bad-boy barn.

"See you, Miles," Hugh called after him, playing his part.

Miles raised his limp hand without turning around. Sarah winked and smiled at Hugh before he got in his car and drove off. When he was out of sight of the farmhouse, Hugh turned off the road into a small clearing in the trees. He parked the Audi where it couldn't be seen from the road, got out, and followed the inside treeline of the road back toward Sarah's house.

Twilight had faded enough so that by the time he reached the long driveway to the house he couldn't be distinguished in the dark. Still, the openness would reveal movement plain enough. He kept in the thickness of the trees and walked past the entrance until he reached the woods that bordered Sarah's field. He crossed the town access road and moved into the bordering forest.

Slow going. The woods were dark and dead pine branches at face level could jab out an eye or gouge his cheeks. He moved through them with his forearms raised in front of his head.

Opposite the farmhouse, he stopped and studied the hundred yards of tall grassy field. A new moon kept the night light down. He pictured himself running crouched across the field, and he heard in his mind's ear Sarah's disgruntled jab at Miles for not cutting the field sooner. The tall grass would hide him.

Sarah had turned out all the lights. The house squatted in the far darkness, a black-on-black shadow against a wash of dark woods on the other side of it.

Hugh ran across the field as low as he could, as fast as he could. When he reached the house, he slid down the outside wall next to the back porch. He listened to his breath and waited for it to calm. Nothing stirred. Nothing made a sound in the night.

He stood up, slipped around the corner of the house, and stretched his long legs two steps at a time up the back porch stairs. The back door was unlatched. He pushed it open, waited, pushed it open farther. And waited again.

He stepped into the kitchen, creaked a floorboard, stopped, let his eyes adjust further to the darker shade of black.

"I'm here," Sarah whispered from a high-back ladder chair in the shrouded corner.

"I couldn't see you," Hugh whispered back.

"That's good, isn't it?"

Good old Sarah.

She stood up and tiptoed to Hugh. "This way."

He followed her through the swinging kitchen door to the living room. "Over there," she directed Hugh, and then she took her assigned seat.

Sarah sat in an upholstered wingback chair next to a tall bookcase. She was stationed obliquely opposite the Dunlap high chest and facing it but half hidden by the bookcase. Hugh sat to her left and next to a glass-door china cabinet that half hid him in the same way.

They sat there in the darkness and silence. The room was nearly pitch black, except for maverick splinters of starlight angling through the gaps between the shades and windowsills, too slight to show the two of them sitting there.

They sat like that for ten minutes.

"How long?" Sarah whispered.

"Anytime. Maybe hours."

"You want me to keep quiet, don't you?"

"Yes."

The house creaked through the long minutes of the night. Rafters snapped from the cold autumn shrink in temperature. Door frames shifted microscopically and sounded the settling. The refrigerator hummed its way through the chilling cycle until it clicked off. Silence and darkness amplified wayward sounds as Hugh and Sarah sat in their chairs and waited and listened.

The longer Hugh waited, the more intensely he listened for the sounds that didn't fit the pattern of the shifting house and its mechanics. Yet the pattern was so irregular in the first place that each snap and crack and click could have been the aberration he was listening for, the announcement of stealth and intrusion.

Of course, another terrifying possibility loomed ahead: the thief might not forewarn them with any sign at all.

For two hours Hugh and Sarah waited in the stillness, listening to their own breaths and pulses against their wills. Maybe Sarah would guess it, but Hugh knew for sure that the house was being watched, studied for lights and move-ment. He gave it another hour, maybe two. In easy weather like this, another hour didn't matter to a cautious killer-thief making sure the house had only Sarah sleeping inside.

Another hour passed in the unmoving dark. Hugh's need to make his own sound and movement pressed against the absolute necessity of watchful silence and still-ness. He must let the sound and movement come to them.

And so they waited.

The creak that came at last from the rear of the house was too unnatural, too deliberate and directed to be from the house itself: the house was reacting to something. Someone.

Hugh listened to what he couldn't see.

Sarah was perfect. She said nothing. Didn't move.

He pictured the back porch and couldn't connect any-thing with the sound. Maybe a raccoon. A raccoon never made sly noises—in the country *or* city. Once a coon started prowling, it kept on prowling, scratching, nudging, climbing.

He waited, his insides now tight as his ears.

The creak came from the kitchen. The floorboard. Hugh'd done the same thing. Loud enough if someone was listening for it, but not for a sleeping old woman three rooms away.

Now he knew what the faint rush of air across his cheeks and hands meant. The back kitchen door was open. And had been left open. The breeze was being sucked through the house by a window open on the other side of the living room, maybe in the dining room or one of the bedrooms down the hall. The air kept flowing: the door had been left open to have it ready for getting away.

The unpredictable occurred to him: was Sarah asleep? He peered at her across the blurry blackness. No, he could see through the scrim of black film that seemed to hang in the room. Her head was erect, alert. He couldn't hear her

159

breaths. She was cool as a cucumber, sitting still with a shawl wrapped over her shoulders against the encroaching cold. She was ready. She knew what to do.

He was counting on her in more ways than one, and she didn't know it. That was the risk. This was her house, and a thief in the night in her home was outrageous, enough to flare her up into an outburst of anger and shrieks. Hugh had to trust the mettle in her. And he had to avoid random thoughts.

He pictured the shadow in the kitchen moving from the back door to the center table, moving like a slippery, bodiless presence, easing to the swinging door between the kitchen and the dining room.

When the door was pressed forward, its spring hinges creaked once, almost imperceptibly. It was a test. The door moved again, and creaked again, and stopped. The noises were barely audible, certainly not enough for a sleeping old woman to hear. But no chances were taken.

After a half minute the door was pressed open more, wider, and this time Hugh felt the rush of a breeze against his face and hands, a more subtle rush of air from the open back door.

The dividing wall between the dining room and living room cut his view of the kitchen door behind the long table and high-back chairs. The thief had to move around the table to get to the living room. Hugh would see the sneak if the shadow moved to the left.

But it didn't. When the swinging door was open body-wide, the silhouette slipped into the dining room like a dark breath. Hugh lost sight of the blur of black in the darkened house as the thief moved around the table to the right, toward the front of the house, away from the hallway that led to the bedroom where Sarah was supposed to be, away from the possibility of making an inadvertent noise too close to the sleeping old woman.

This thief probably would have no gun ready for a sleeping old woman. Hugh was also banking on the thief's desperate focus on the high chest, so that any excited breath that came from himself or Sarah wouldn't be heard. The house was too dark to distinguish anything more than undecipherable outlines. But Hugh and Sarah had had the advantage of hours to adjust their eyes and wills.

The thief was slinking around the table now, out of sight of Hugh, but when the figure came clear of the dividing wall Hugh could see the caution in the silhouette as it stepped forward, catlike, froze to listen, then slipped on toward the chest standing against the center wall of the living room.

The urge to snap the spring on the trap grew almost irresistible as Hugh watched the thief tiptoe across the rug, a big shadow stepping like a dainty child. When the floor creaked under the carpet, the figure froze in half-step until enough silence filled the gap to move again.

Hugh might have been wrong in exposing Sarah to this danger, but her presence was essential for what she would do when the time came.

Don't think about grave errors, he told himself, but he couldn't help it. The viciousness of the shadow stealing into her house, trespassing her safety, mocked his own mammoth inaction as he sat there watching the progress of this crime. Hugh held himself back from the compulsion to pummel the sneak thief and ruin it all.

The shadow thief stood in front of the high chest now and reached up to the left drawer of the top row. The figure lifted the brass handle in slow motion—carefully, noiselessly—and then pulled the drawer outward, inch by inch. The scraping noise of the old construction forced the thief to pull slowly.

When the drawer was clear of the chest, the thief took it in both hands and eased it down the rug, crouching like a black turtle.

Then the blurry shadow stood upright again and froze,

161

looking to the hallway, listening for any sign that these sounds might have roused the sleeping old woman who owned the house that was being burglarized. Nothing. Total silence.

That total silence was what alarmed Hugh the most. The longer the thief was watched, the more surely the sense of it would fill the room. Eventually, he was bound to feel the presence of others in the room—Hugh's and Sarah's flesh and bones emanating heat across the room that pressed in on the thief's own alerted presence.

Hugh prayed for the thief to go one, irretrievably convicting step further. He knew now that this midnight skulker was more attuned to the unseen presence of others in the forest outdoors than in a wooden house.

The thief heard and sensed nothing. He turned back to the chest and reached up to the empty space where he had removed the drawer. He stretched his right hand inside, angling his elbow high and unnaturally. The quiet scrape of his hands and fingers kept on longer than Hugh and Sarah would have thought.

Then suddenly the panel beneath the bonnet cornice flipped down and open. The thief reached into the hidden compartment, patted around for the unseen contents, and withdrew the two envelopes.

This was the trip wire that Hugh and Sarah had been waiting for, the move that signaled to both of them the rest of their so simple plan. They had already set up everyone about the schedule for moving the chest out of Sarah's house into storage the next day, and they had set the house up for easy entry. They had even filled the high chest full of ripe bait, and now was the time for the next signal, for Hugh to say what he knew but what Sarah did not yet know.

"Hi, Toop."

The words broke through the blackness like loud cracking ice. Hugh's steady, calm voice thundered through the room, and an instant later Sarah, on the other side of the room, flicked the wall switch next to her, flooding the room with light.

The thief froze, paralyzed, totally nailed to the light. The secret envelopes in his paws. Panic in his eyes.

And then Sarah came through with what Hugh had counted on. She was the bloody fight substituted, the gunfire and fists and wounds eliminated. She was his easy collar of the thief. Her outrage came to a head and crushed the thief and killer right in place, right in front of her shocked old woman's face that overpowered this found and confounded old man. She made him have nowhere to go, and no will to go if he had.

"Toop!" she shouted, wide-eyed, truly shocked and unbelieving, truly powerful against the betrayal of friend and neighbor. "It's you! Toop Tucker, you should be *ashamed* of yourself!"

20

THINKING TO GET AT ONCE ALL THE GOLD
THE GOOSE COULD GIVE, HE KILLED IT AND
OPENED IT ONLY TO FIND — NOTHING.

—AESOP

HUGH REPLACED THE phone receiver and then said, "You killed Bryan, didn't you, Toop?"

Toop pressed himself against the wall next to the Dunlap high chest. His gut caved into his spine, his shoulders half folded over as if he were recovering from a slug in his stomach. He said nothing.

Sarah stared at the crumpled man.

"You killed Bryan," Hugh said, "because as Sarah's lawyer he had her original will in his files in the vault. At first that's what I thought you were after. But it wasn't, was it?"

Toop stared at him from under his creased eyebrows.

"It was the bill of sale you wanted," Hugh continued, "not the will. So you stabbed Bryan and stole Sarah's file from his vault. Only the bill of sale wasn't in Sarah's file. Who knows how you got Bryan to open the vault. It was probably some friendly suggestion and curiosity. You and Bryan and Danny Mayes were playing poker, weren't you? I saw the cards in Bryan's drawer."

"Poor Danny," Sarah said.

"When you realized that Sarah had stipulated in her will that the chest was to be returned to you and Zeta, it was already too late," Hugh said. "You'd killed Bryan. But now

164

Danny was too close to the scene and he could have pieced things together. You had to get rid of him. So you got him out there in the woods on some phony pretext. Why wouldn't he meet you out there? You were his friend. Or maybe he had some suspicions about you and was blackmailing you. I doubt that, though. You clubbed him and hanged him."

Toop said nothing.

Hugh glanced at Sarah and went on. "You covered up your tracks. You had to get that bill of sale, only Bryan had given it to Sarah. He'd put a note in her file along with the will saying that the bill of sale for the chest was in the secret compartment in the chest, along with the copy of the will. Sarah put the copy there because she wanted Miles and Amy to think that the chest would always be in the family. She didn't want anybody to see the actual will, because she really wanted the Dunlap returned to you and Zeta. But with the bill of sale out of the way, you could work on getting the chest right away. You could sue for it, and she wouldn't have any documents for it. Was that it, Toop?"

He said nothing.

"Nobody told Sarah about that hidden drawer," Hugh said. "Not you or Zeta, and you two would be the ones to know and tell her when Eddie won the chest. But neither one of you was about to tell her anything."

"Eddie found it," Sarah said. "He knew these old chests had them and so one day he spent all afternoon looking for it, and he found it."

"So when Sarah's bill of sale was missing and you saw that note about where it was, you knew where to look," Hugh said. "Nobody else could have known about that note, except Zeta, and that wasn't likely."

"When you found out what I really wanted to do, why didn't you just quit that killing, for heaven's sakes?" Sarah asked.

Toop stared at her.

Killing didn't work that way, Hugh wanted to tell her. "Then Frank Ritter got in the way," he said. "Someone else's greed moved in and Ritter almost stole the Dunlap right out from under you. It enraged you, didn't it, Toop? A total stranger, a thug, coming in and stealing the chest right out from under your nose, and after all you'd done to get at it. You knew Ritter would try again, and maybe succeed. So you followed him, and then when I got caught in it you followed me following him. It all worked out. You knew what to do, and you could do it. You could even ransack my cabin and shove me into the door—and get away with it."

"It was just a high chest," Sarah said, shaking her head.

"Not anymore," Hugh said. "In the old days, Sarah, it was just a chest. But with all the high pressure from antique dealers siphoning off the old furniture around here, shipping it out to Texas and California, the prices went up. It was still the same old chest, but the prices weren't. A signed Dunlap like yours fetches big money. Toop knew that. Didn't you? Maybe a hundred thousand dollars."

No answer.

But Sarah turned to Hugh at the mention of so much money.

"If he could get that bill of sale, Sarah, he could maybe sue you for the chest and get it back legally," Hugh said, "and then sell it."

"Why didn't you just wait until I died, Toop?" Sarah asked, her words reflecting the disbelief inside her.

When Toop turned to her but said nothing, Hugh said the obvious: "Sarah, the way you're going you could live forever." He glanced at Toop, and this time the man looked back with acknowledgment that Hugh was right.

"After all these years," Sarah said, shaking her head again. "Why now, Toop? Why now?"

Hugh waited for Toop to answer. When he didn't, Hugh

said, "Eric was convenient. Eric isn't liked much for what he's doing, and everybody around here knows that he always greets people with, 'Welcome to our mountains.' So Toop made sure the killings connected with Eric in some way like that. And, of course, everybody knew about Eric and Amy and how everybody thought he had stolen Amy from Calvin. You used what was there, didn't you, Toop?"

"Poor Calvin," Sarah said. "Did you ever think of him?"

Hugh waited. Toop didn't answer but a tightness narrowed his eyes and strained the muscles at his jaw and in his neck.

"He thought about it the other way, Sarah. He thought it was all going to work out, and if it did Eric would be blamed. Calvin would get Amy back, and Zeta would get the chest back."

Sarah sighed. "I just don't know. Poor Zeta."

"Poor Zeta?" Toop exploded. "Zeta? Years she blames me for that chest. Every day she screams at me for years! Get the chest back, she screams, get the chest back. It's my chest, she says, it's the Tucker Dunlap, she says. Get it back, get it back. She screams it at me! Every day! Yeah, well, she thought it *was* Eric doing the killing, killing a lawyer who'd fight him, killing Danny in our woods to make it look like we did it, killing that punk in the mountains like an *Indian* would. Ha! Mrs. Smart-Ass Woman couldn't tell the difference. Yelling at me all the time—get it back, get it back. Fifteen years she yells it at me. Fifteen years!"

The words showed the magma of anger boiling inside him. They weren't enough to steam the fury away. Toop Tucker, the rough-hewn, big-pawed mountain man, swelled like a fantasy monster against the pressure of outrage and resentment. His eyes whitened from the interior flame that burned him. His breath shortened and bellowed out, and in the frightening seconds that followed, the conflagration inside him blazed through his limbs, fierce and clawing.

The detonation roared from his mouth: "Aaggggggghhh!"

He turned and arched his back. Then, with bared teeth and the power of hate for the conspiracy of the whole cosmos that entangled him, he shoved the Dunlap high chest with all his inflamed might. It slid and tipped and finally tumbled onto its face, drawers sliding out until the angle of the crash and the weight of the falling structure crunched them beneath it, a colossus of glory shattered.

Chief Maddox left the blue lights whirling as he parked his patrol car and got out to meet Hugh, Sarah, and Toop Tucker on the front steps.

Hugh told the chief what had happened and that Toop would have something to talk to him about later. The chief said that he'd ask Hugh and Sarah to make statements. They said of course. The chief didn't have the sad look that Sarah wore when Toop got into the back seat of the patrol car. He hadn't known Toop his whole life the way she had.

The chief got behind the wheel, shifted into reverse, backed up a little, shifted again, and circled around onto the driveway, then out to the road. He kept the blue lights whirling. He wasn't much of an old-timer yet.

Miles came running from the barn. "Hey! What's going on here? Who's that?"

"Did you fix that coffeepot?" Sarah asked.

"I'm working on it. I'm working on it."

"Miles," Sarah said, "You're such a good boy."

Miles stared at her and then at Hugh. "Is she all right?"

As usual, Proctor Hammond sounded as if he were late for a Cape Canaveral blast-off. "Speak."

"Such charm. Such an air of bon vivant."

"So it's Quint again. I might have known. When one lifts the phone off the hook one must expect anything and everything. One must be open to the gamut of surprises, whether one learns from these encounters or not. One must be tolerant."

168

"One must."

"I take it that you have inquiries to make about that sleazy episode of murder and mayhem up there in them thar northern wilds."

"Not anymore."

"Really," Proctor said, genuinely surprised. The report almost silenced him. "Either you survived, or this must be a prerecorded message."

Hugh told him about the trap he had set with Sarah.

"I'm very impressed, Quint. But what took you so long? A Toop Tucker-type of man can chop down hundred-foot spruces for a quarter century. He can plunder a forest forever, move mountains by the mapful, climb Mt. Washington with a single bound, but when it comes to dealing with his harpy wife, fifteen years is the limit. It's a wonder five weeks wasn't the limit. That's why a man like Toop Tucker is in the woods in the first place. Dealing with trees is much easier than dealing with Zetas."

"Why Proctor, that's a very human analysis. I'm amazed."

"The turncoat Boston Brahmin mocks me with no effect whatsoever. I, at least, perform my job to the fullest."

"And what's that supposed to mean?"

"You are bathing in peripheral glory, Quint. All right, so you solved a triple murder and sort of saved a valuable piece of antiquity from black-market hijacking and probable disappearance. At least it can be repaired—remember that $30,000 Stradivarius I told you about—and you saved a town from ransacking its heritage and blaming the wrong person, even the wrong civilization. But you didn't do what you were supposed to do."

"Oh?"

"You didn't find Amy."

Then, of course, Proctor Hammond said nothing else, to let his words soak in.

"Amy is all right."

"You know that?"

"I know that from those who know. Besides, Sarah isn't worried about her that much anymore."

"Then she isn't her mother."

"Touché, Proctor. The fact of the matter is that Eric and Amy are bigger than themselves and that's the difference. They've got a cause that makes them safe for each other."

"Just so you know the source of your glory, Quint. That's *my* mission. Exactitude. Facts. No ricochet luminescence for the undeserving. England had only one *Great* king and that was Alfred. Hugh Quint the Great doesn't make it for America."

"Are you suggesting Proctor Hammond the Great?"

"You're the one who said it."

"Isn't Hammond an organ?"

"Right. The brain."

If you have enjoyed this book and would like to receive details of other Walker Mystery-Suspense Novels, or join our *Crime After Crime* Book Club please write to:

Mystery-Suspense Editor
Walker and Company
720 Fifth Avenue
New York, NY 10019